After having been illegally experimented on by a shadow branch of the military bent on creating the perfect super soldier, Ulrick Lanston needed a place to relearn himself. Not only did they bond him with a massive jaguar, allowing him to turn into the cat at will, they'd messed with his brain, taking away his free will. After losing his handler and ending up at loose ends, Ulrick tracked down an old army acquaintance he could trust. That led him to Alpha Declan's wolf shifter pack, and he's been hiding out with them for over a year. They've helped him come to grips with the changes made to him, teaching him how to become one with the animal now living within him.

When Alpha Declan asks Ulrick to sneak into the territory of a coyote shifter pack to look for a missing pack member, he can't say no. While doing reconnaissance, Ulrick runs across the prettiest coyote he's ever seen. His jaguar wants to rub all over the wonderful-smelling shifter, marking him as his own. Ulrick knows what that means. His cat has decided the coyote is his mate.

Can Ulrick win the affections of the skittish coyote shifter and bring him home with him while still fulfilling his mission for Declan?

Cuddling with a Coyote

ISBN: 978-1-4874-3935-4
Cover art by Angela Waters

Published by eXtasy Books Inc

Look for us online at:
www.eXtasybooks.com

Cuddling with a Coyote
Wolves of Stone Ridge 61

By

Charlie Richards

Dedication

Family means no one gets left behind or forgotten.
~David Ogden Stiers

Chapter One

"Thank ye for agreein' to help, Ulrick," Alpha Declan McIntire rumbled. His lightly Irish-accented voice softened, turning serious. "It's a delicate matter, and I can't just claim foul play without proof."

Ulrick Lanston nodded once. "I'm happy to help, Alpha," he replied. Resting his coffee mug on his thigh, he eyed the large black man who shared his psyche with a huge wolf and could turn into the animal at will. "You and your people have done so much for me in the past year. It's my honor to be able to repay you and yours in some small way."

"Helping ye has been our honor," Declan countered, even as his expression hardened. "What General Sackett did to you and others is beyond despicable," he stated on a growl, his countenance darkening. "May the gods have mercy on the souls who didn't make it through the process."

Ulrick blinked, having not even considered that.

How many good men died being experimented on before the rogue science division figured out how to splice shifter DNA into a human?

For nearly eight years, Ulrick had been proud to be in the military. He'd worked hard and risen through the special forces ranks, becoming elite at black ops, often getting the opportunity to cherry-pick his crew for whatever assignment he'd been given. Ulrick couldn't remember much of the assignment that had left him with life-threatening injuries, sending him to Doctor Winoan's lab.

Memories of his years working under General Sackett as a

zombie-like soldier—doing exactly what he was told and only what he was told—were hazy at best. Only recalling certain dates allowed him to piece together how long he'd been under the general's control—*over six years.* Considering the bits Ulrick could recall—things that surfaced mostly in his dreams—he felt he was better off not knowing.

Ulrick had been out on assignment with his handler—a man he knew only as Sir Lentz—when General Sackett had disappeared. He knew now that the general was in the custody of the CIA. Sir Lentz had ordered Ulrick to remain in their motel room until he returned.

The man hadn't returned, and Ulrick had nearly died from lack of food and water trying to follow that order. Fortunately, his survival abilities—ingrained in him from years of training and missions—had kicked in. Coupled with the lack of daily injections that had suppressed his shifter side, waking his jaguar's instincts, Ulrick had slowly begun thinking for himself—food and shelter being at the top of his muddled brain's priorities.

After several months of living alone in the woods, feeding off the land, Ulrick had begun recalling bits and pieces of his past. He'd remembered that he was special forces. He'd remembered a few bases that he'd lived at. Ulrick had also recalled the name of a fellow soldier that he knew he could trust—David Preston.

Ulrick had focused all his energy on tracking down his fellow soldier. To his surprise, David and his unit had also fallen prey to General Sackett. Their leader, however—Bailey Dyer—had escaped the complete process when his older brother, Ronan, had whisked him away from the facility.

Ronan had stumbled upon the wolf shifters, who'd not only believed his tales, but they'd dealt with similar issues in the past. The shifters had taken up the crusade of ridding the world of General Sackett and Doctor Winoan's despicable activities. While Ulrick wasn't part of the process, he knew the wolves felt they were nearly there, too.

When Ulrick had arrived in Stone Ridge—a small town tucked in the Colorado mountains and within Alpha Declan's territory, which also gave them their name-sake—he'd discovered that he wasn't the only one sneaking into the area. He'd revealed himself to David just enough to alarm the other soldier, putting the pack on alert. They'd caught the other guys, and Ulrick gained their help in figuring out his knew reality.

A new reality where I share my mind with that of a jaguar and can turn into that large cat at will.

Still strange to think about.

Tuning back in to what Alpha Declan was saying, Ulrick refocused on the alpha wolf shifter. He needed information, after all, if he were to help the man find his missing member.

"Two weeks ago, Jocomo went to visit his family in the coyote pack south of us," Alpha Declan told him. "He's supposed to check in every third day with my pack's liaison, Cayden Rochette. Cayden informed me this morning that Jocomo has missed his last two check-ins."

While curiosity wasn't something Ulrick had indulged in in the past, he found bonding with a cat had changed that. He'd always thought the quip about curiosity killing the cat was just a saying. That wasn't the case for the animal he now shared his psyche with. Ulrick's beast loved exploring his forest home and sniffing at every new scent he came across.

Ulrick's new-found curiosity had to be the reason he interrupted Alpha Declan, asking, "Jocomo is a wolf shifter, but his family lives with coyote shifters?" Tipping his head to the side a little, Ulrick mused, "Does that happen often?"

The corners of Alpha Declan's lips twitched, and the lines of frustration there eased. "It happens often enough," he told him. After a second of hesitation, Declan explained, "Jocomo's mother is a wolf shifter. A pretty submissive one, from what Jocomo's told me. His father's a coyote shifter and runs the house." After taking a sip of his own coffee, Declan told him, "Due to that, when they mated, I doubt anyone was surprised when they ended up living in the father's coyote pack."

Nodding slowly, Ulrick thought he understood. "So, their offspring could be a wolf shifter or a coyote shifter?" When he saw Declan nodding, he murmured, "I wonder how that's determined."

Declan shrugged. "Only the Fates know."

Fair enough.

Ulrick set his empty mug aside before straightening in his seat. "So Jocomo was born there, but left his birth pack to join yours at some point," he guessed.

Nodding once more, Declan told him, "Jocomo joined my pack nearly three decades ago when he needed an identity change." Rubbing a hand over his bald pate in clear agitation, he continued to say, "With how long he's been here, Jocomo's due for another identity. He's using this trip as the start of his nearly ten years of isolation."

"Isolation?" Ulrick racked his brain, trying to recall hearing anything about that sort of thing from David.

If Ulrick had, the memory wasn't surfacing. As frustrating as it was, that happened on occasion. While Ulrick's brain was mostly back to his own, he occasionally lost time, not recalling what he'd been doing or where.

When that happened, Ulrick usually woke in cat form after a nap in a tree.

It was almost as if his other half was protecting him . . . or saving him from returning to the programing the scientists had done to his brain.

"Aye," Declan confirmed. "Because we pretty much stop aging once we hit about thirty, we have to remake our identity every few decades. Otherwise, humans would get suspicious." With a shrug and a wry smile, he told him, "It was so much easier before the invention of electronics and the internet."

"I bet," Ulrick mused in understanding. "So Jocomo went to visit his family, and no one has heard from him in . . . over a week?"

Declan winced. "Exactly." His lips turned up in a snarl as he told him, "And when Cayden contacted the beta there, Beta Friar, he was told that Jocomo had already left, but according to Jocomo, he'd received permission to stay for over a month."

"What do Jocomo's parents say?"

Growling softly, Declan told him, "Cayden doesn't have Jocomo's mother's number, and the father backs up Friar's story."

"But you don't believe them?" Ulrick wondered if Jocomo really had decided to leave early.

"Definitely not," Declan replied, sounding certain. "He would have told Cayden. Besides, Jocomo and his father's relationship was strained because of his sexual orientation."

In Ulrick's mind, that just lent credence to him possibly leaving early. Except, Declan's next words gave him pause.

"One of the reasons Jocomo was planning to spend so much time there was because of his younger brother, Jeremy." Rising to his feet, Declan moved toward the bar. "Jocomo told us that Jeremy is bisexual, but the inner circle is pressuring him to take a wife in order to have pups and increase pack numbers." Grabbing the coffee carafe, Declan began filling his mug as he grumbled, "I hate it when alphas try to force pack members that way." Lifting the carafe, the alpha asked, "Refill?"

Shaking his head, Ulrick rose to his feet. "No, thank you, Alpha." Ready to get started, he asked, "Is there anything else

I should be aware of?"

Declan leaned against the bar after returning the carafe to the warmer. "Stop at Cayden's," he ordered. "He has a dossier ready for you. It'll give you the names of the coyote pack's inner circle, as well as Jocomo's family." Declan pinned Ulrick with a serious look as he added, "There'll also be a map of the territory. Plus, where those people live in relation to the borders."

Understanding, Ulrick stated, "That's good. It'll let me know the easiest route to sneak in."

"Exactly." After a second of hesitation, Alpha Declan added, "Be careful, Ulrick. If ye're found in coyote territory, they will probably be more likely to attack than ask questions."

With a scoff, Ulrick muttered, "Not real friendly, huh?"

Declan shook his head. "Afraid not."

Ulrick tipped his chin down in a brief nod. "Got it."

"And thanks again."

Recognizing a dismissal when he heard it, Ulrick responded, "Again, I'm happy to help." Then he headed toward Alpha Declan's study door, saying over his shoulder, "I'll keep you posted."

"Safe travels, Ulrick."

After another nod, Ulrick headed out the door.

Padding through the forest, Ulrick easily navigated the rough mountain terrain. His paws landed silently on the dirt and pine needles strewn across the forest floor. He listened intently, taking in the sounds of the woodland creatures around him.

When a squirrel rustled overhead, Ulrick felt a small urge to race up the trunk and chase the critter. It would make a tasty mouthful of a snack. He resisted. After all, he wasn't really hungry.

Plus, I have jerky, dried fruit, nuts, and seeds in the backpack I left a mile back.

Ulrick had chosen to creep stealthily into the coyote pack territory in his jaguar form. He knew he would be able to get in and out much faster that way. Plus, if he ran into any problems, he could take to the trees and easily evade the pack that way.

With that plan in mind, Ulrick had left not only his backpack of supplies, but his weapons, too. They were all concealed in a hole in the trunk of a dying pine tree. After figuring out a reasonably safe route to Jocomo's mother's place for him to travel on two legs, Ulrick would return and catch her alone.

Cayden hadn't been certain if Jeremy still lived with his parents or not. The man was nearly eighty years old, but due to the way the housing was set up—almost as if the group lived like a commune—it was possible he hadn't been allowed to leave until he married. When Cayden had visited nearly a decade before to work out new boundaries, he hadn't been allowed to reside in the pack's town proper. Instead, he'd rented a room at a bed and breakfast in the next town over.

The pack stayed to themselves as much as possible—gardening and growing their own crops, as well as hunting for their meat.

According to the couple that had run the bed and breakfast, they were under the impression that the coyote pack was actually a group of religious zealots of some kind.

Cayden hadn't corrected their thinking.

The sound of water rushing over rocks caught Ulrick's attention, confirming his position. Turning toward the noise, he made his way toward the water. He knew if he followed it, it would lead him directly to the coyote pack. The shifters had set up their town half a mile from the river.

After getting a drink from the cool mountain stream, Ulrick leaped to the far bank. He began making his way carefully over the rocky terrain, heading downstream. Reaching the top of a twenty-foot, rocky waterfall, Ulrick peered over the edge, searching for the best way down.

Ulrick's sharp feline sight caught movement below, and he quickly crouched. As he watched, a small coyote trotted from between the trees. The animal's dirty-blond and gray coat gleamed in the sunlight, and Ulrick found his attention entranced by the pretty creature.

Wait a second. Pretty?

Barely resisting his urge to rumble a soft purr of appreciation, Ulrick tensed in the bushes. If he could have, he would have mentally slapped his jaguar upside the head. Except, he barely felt in control when his beast tipped his head up and sniffed, trying to catch the scent of the coyote currently drinking from the pool below.

An earthy, masculine scent with a hint of canine teased his senses. His cat found the smell delicious, and Ulrick's mouth began to water. Instead of a desire to catch and eat the small canine, he had the unmistakable need to rub against the beast, to share in his scent.

Realization hit Ulrick.

Well, shit. That little coyote is my mate.

With a mental groan, Ulrick knew that his jaguar would refuse to cooperate if he attempted to let the little shifter get away. He'd never been in a relationship before—the military had been his mistress. Ulrick had scratched his itch with a like-minded man or woman when he felt the desire to get his rocks off.

Regardless, Ulrick knew that was about to change.

For better or worse, that little coyote is now mine.

Accepting what his jaguar was insisting, Ulrick plotted a course down the waterfall, intent on capturing his prey.

Chapter Two

Settling on his belly, Taylor rested his head on his paws. He relaxed, allowing his eyelids to slide to half-mast. Taylor knew he couldn't dally for long, but for a few minutes, he was going to allow himself a moment of peace and quiet.

Taylor loved running in his fur, but he knew he would be missed if he took too long. Alpha Stewart would be expecting his dinner soon, after all. If Taylor was late taking him his bowl of stew and fresh-baked bread, his back would feel it for days.

Still, with the sound of the water rushing over the rocks lulling his senses, Taylor allowed himself this short indulgence. He wondered what it would be like to live in a different coyote pack. Taylor had to believe that not all packs were run like this one—where the weak were forced to serve the strong.

Unfortunately, Taylor had been born into the pack. When it had been run by Alpha Regan, it had been a fairly nice place to live. Taylor had had a part-time job in town, and he'd been able to interact with humans.

Then Beta Arden had shown his true colors—going against Alpha Regan's decision to trade away some of their pack territory to a wolf shifter pack up north. Beta Arden had snuck into wolf territory with a couple of enforcers, and he'd attacked the shifter negotiator. Beta Arden had been caught and killed.

While Alpha Regan hadn't been involved, losing Arden

had still impacted him. The beta had been stronger than Regan, and when he'd lost the shifter's backing, it had left their coyote pack open to outside attack. A trio of assholes had taken over the inner circle—Alpha Stewart, Beta Friar, and the new head enforcer, Kris.

The trio had made a lot of changes in the last several years, including demanding that all of the weaker pack members quit their jobs. Taylor had essentially become a slave to the trio, cleaning the pack house, serving their meals, and completing whatever menial tasks they ordered. At least he hadn't been ordered to marry some poor girl in order to breed more pups for the pack. Taylor felt sorry for those that had been forced into that situation.

Plus, I wouldn't know what to do with a woman anyway.

Taylor had known he was gay from the age of twelve. Unfortunately, that was another thing that had changed when the trio took over. Being gay was no longer allowed.

Taylor's small size had one thing going for him. While he was essentially a slave to the inner circle, they didn't want him to breed. He was too small and weak. They didn't want his genetics passed on.

Thank the gods for small favors.

Knowing his short quiet time was over, Taylor let out a quiet huff. He began lifting his head, preparing to rise, when a large dark shadow fell over him. For a second, he feared that one of the inner circle had found him, and he would be beaten for lazing about. Except, then a scent Taylor had never smelled before flooded his nostrils—something decidedly feline and masculine and oh-so-wonderful.

Snapping his head around, Taylor gaped, even in coyote form. A large jaguar was easing over his much smaller frame. Taylor could only stare, frozen in shock, as the strange shifter lowered his head and rubbed his cheek over his head.

A second later, the jaguar stuck out his tongue and licked over Taylor's head next.

Taylor wanted to whimper with pleasure as the jaguar began coating him with his scent.

My mate. Oh gods, he's my mate. And he's marking me.

Then Taylor realized something else—when he returned to the pack, everyone would be able to smell it.

Shit!

With the large cat crouched over him, Taylor knew he couldn't flee. In truth, he didn't want to, either. He wanted his fated mate just as much as the next person.

Unfortunately, Taylor knew that there was no way the big jaguar would be welcomed into his coyote pack. Not only would the inner circle try to kill him simply for being in their territory, but for obviously being gay, as well. While Taylor hadn't been in the closet before they'd taken over, no one spoke of his orientation after.

Needing to explain the situation, Taylor initiated his shift. As he changed, he hoped the fact that the big cat was licking his coyote would mean that he could recognize him in human form. He also hoped the male would take it as his cue to shift, too.

While Taylor had never had the fastest shift in the world, he didn't think he was slow either. That was why when he opened his human eyes to peer at the jaguar, surprise filled him. The man had already completed his shift, and Taylor stared into intense black eyes that looked nothing like the green ones the jaguar had.

"H-Hi," Taylor whispered, suddenly feeling shy. "I-I'm Taylor."

"Hello, Taylor," the man replied, the corners of his lips twitching just a little. "I'm Ulrick."

"Ulrick," Taylor repeated softly, enjoying the unfamiliar name. In response, Ulrick tipped his chin in a slight nod. "Um, nice to meet you."

Ulrick lowered his bulk until his chest pressed against Taylor's back. "You, too, Taylor," he rumbled before sniffing openly. "Mmmm, you do smell good."

With Ulrick's heavy frame pressed against him, Taylor nearly forgot why he'd shifted in the first place. He felt the man's thick erection pressed against his thigh, and his breath caught in his throat. A shudder of answering need rushed through Taylor's body, his own prick twitching at his groin.

When Ulrick threaded his fingers in Taylor's hair, scratching at his scalp in a sensual massage, Taylor let out a low moan.

"Yeah," Ulrick muttered, rocking his hips, rutting against him. "That's a pleasant sound." His voice lowered to a guttural growl as he murmured, "Could get used to hearing it damn fast."

"U-Ulrick," Taylor whimpered, desperately wanting to roll to his back so he could get a little friction on his own shaft.

"That's right," Ulrick crooned, sliding his other arm under Taylor's body. While he kept his weight on that arm, he also used it to clutch Taylor tighter against his chest. "Feel what you do to me, my mate."

Grinding against him harder, Ulrick lowered his head and began mouthing along his collarbone, and Taylor instinctively tipped his head to the side, offering more room.

"Such sweet submission," Ulrick whispered. "Never imagined it could feel like this." After a nip to Taylor's flesh, he muttered, "Gonna spill on you, Taylor. Mark you as mine." Releasing Taylor's hair, Ulrick slipped that hand under Taylor's waist. "You gonna come from my bite, Taylor?"

As Ulrick finished speaking, he wrapped thick, calloused fingers around Taylor's shaft. He jacked him slowly, creating the most delicious wash of tingles along the sensitive skin of his erection. The sensations moved swiftly to Taylor's balls, and he felt them tighten.

"Ready?" Ulrick growled, his sharp teeth pricking Taylor's shoulder.

The sting caused Taylor's nipples to bead, and his coyote howled eagerly in his mind. Even though he knew nothing about the man holding him, he wanted that bond so damn badly. Taylor could finally leave his shitty pack and—

Wait. Pack.

"Wait, wait," Taylor cried breathlessly. He felt the teeth lift from his neck, creating a crashing disappointment within him. Still, Taylor had to get the words out. "If you mark me, my pack will smell it. They'll know."

"Yes, they will," Ulrick stated, his voice deep and calm. While his hips and the hand he used to jack Taylor's erection had slowed, he hadn't stopped entirely. "I thought shifters liked knowing that they're marked by their fated mate. It's a matter of pride for you, isn't it?"

"W-Well, yeah," Taylor responded, panting softly as he processed Ulrick's oddly spoken words. "Wh-What do you m-mean by, uh, that? You're a shifter, too."

"I was born human," Ulrick claimed.

"What?" Taylor squeaked, craning his neck so he could peer back at the man more fully. "That's not possible."

"It's true," Ulrick countered, and when he continued speaking, Taylor openly sniffed him, learning his mate believed what he claimed. "I've only been a shifter for a few years."

"How?" Taylor couldn't help but ask, shaking his head in shock.

"That's a tale for another time, Taylor," Ulrick told him. A growl returned to his voice as he rocked his hips harder. "Tell me why you stopped me from starting our claim?"

"Because my pack won't accept us," Taylor explained, even as his body flushed hot with continued arousal. Ulrick still had a hand on his cock, and his fondling felt so fantastic. "Alpha Stewart will have us killed."

"For finding your fated mate?" Ulrick asked incredulously, anger darkening his scent.

"For being gay," Taylor corrected. "When they took over several years ago, I was forced into the closet."

"Good thing we won't be staying here, then," Ulrick declared. "We'll sneak into your pack, get what you need, find Jocomo, and get the hell out of here."

As Ulrick spoke, he began speeding up his movements once more.

Taylor moaned, pushing back into Ulrick's body before popping his hips forward, pushing into his fated mate's grip. He wanted to ask all sorts of questions, but his brain was starting to shut down with the pleasurable sensations Ulrick was easily ringing from his body. Taylor knew it wouldn't be as easy as his new and forever lover's words, but he couldn't manage to get the warning past his lips.

With his need to come consuming him, Taylor only managed to mutter, "Don't bite me, yet."

While Ulrick let out a growl, expressing his displeasure at the order, he tucked his forehead against Taylor's neck, obviously intending to obey.

Ulrick twisted the arm under Taylor, brushing his fingers over his nipple. A second later, he gripped the hardened nub and pinched lightly. The jolt of pleasure-pain went straight to Taylor's gut.

Barking Ulrick's name, Taylor felt his balls pull tight. He groaned deeply as his release caused his body to flush hot. Fiery tendrils of bliss washed over Taylor's senses as he unloaded his seed into the grass beneath him, and his mind floated in ecstasy.

Taylor wasn't certain how long he remained tucked against Ulrick's hard body. When he came back to himself, he realized the man had adjusted them. They lay on their left sides with Ulrick spooned behind him. Their legs were tangled together, and the much larger man held him close while nuzzling his goatee against his nape.

Something must have alerted Ulrick that Taylor was with it again, for he chuckled softly before saying, "You back with me, Taylor?"

"Mmm-hmmm," Taylor confirmed. With a sigh, he muttered, "Wow."

Ulrick chuckled again. "You must have needed that."

Taylor snickered. "Something like that." Turning a bit in Ulrick's arms, he met the other man's gaze. "Been a while would be an understatement. In the closet for years and not allowed off pack lands." Then he frowned and admitted, "And I don't want to hear about when the last time you had sex with someone."

Scoffing softly, Ulrick sobered. "Well, it's been years for me, too."

Gaping, Taylor couldn't hide his disbelief. The man holding him was big, sexy, and drop-dead gorgeous. He bet the man could have his choice of, well, anyone.

But he's mine now.

Ulrick offered him a small smile. "That's part of the *being turned into a shifter* story," he told him. Then he frowned and lifted his head. "And we're going to have company soon. I hear the sound of paws."

"Shit," Taylor squeaked, jerking forward. "You need to go," he claimed, trying to pull from Ulrick's arms.

"Where the hell do you think I'm going to go without my mate?" Ulrick growled, tightening his hold. "We're a team now, Taylor. Have you forgotten that already?"

"I haven't forgotten," Taylor assured, managing to turn in Ulrick's hold. He gripped one of his big lover's wrists and squeezed lightly. "If we're found together by my alpha, beta, or one of the enforcers, they'll try to kill us," Taylor reminded him. Then he lowered his voice to a whisper, as he could now make out the sound of an approaching coyote, too. "And if they know you're here, you'll never manage to free Jocomo."

Evidently, reminding Ulrick of why he was there did the

trick. With a snarl, he released Taylor. The big man was on his feet in an instant, offering his hand to help Taylor up.

"I'm a servant in the alpha's house," Taylor explained, wincing as he felt the evidence of Ulrick's release begin to drip down his back. Quickly, Taylor stuck his hand behind him to catch it, so it didn't drop on the grass. "I'm supposed to be serving the inner circle their dinner right now." Taylor hurried toward the river, carefully stepping into the chilly water. "That's probably someone sent to find me." Dipping into the water, Taylor began wiping away the evidence of Ulrick's release . . . as well as his mate's scent. "I'll sneak out after they go to bed and meet you," Taylor told his scowling mate. "Then I'll take you to where they're holding Jocomo."

A muscle ticked in Ulrick's jaw, and his fingers clenched and released at his side. A low growl rumbled from his chest, but he stopped it quickly enough. His attention snapped to the trees to the right.

"I'll be watching you, Taylor," Ulrick rumbled quietly.

A second later, Ulrick shifted.

Taylor gaped as between one second and the next, where a man had stood, there was a massive jaguar instead. The large animal stared at him with vibrant, intelligent green eyes. The jaguar's ear twitched once. Then he turned and disappeared amidst the trees.

"Holy shit," Taylor whispered as he continued to wash himself. "Never seen anyone shift that fast."

Spotting a gray coyote appear from between trees, Taylor pretended not to see him. He ducked under the water, submerging himself fully. After a quick rub over every bit of his skin, doing his best to ignore the goose bumps, Taylor broke the surface once more.

On the bank stood a naked man.

"Hey, Marc," Taylor greeted, adding an inflection of surprise to his voice. "What's up?"

"Do you know what time it is?" Marc asked, grimacing.

Glancing at the sky, Taylor pretended to guess based on the sun's position. "Ah, shit," he muttered. Letting out a deep sigh, he exited the water. "It's later than I thought. Am I in trouble?"

"Not yet." Marc offered him a rueful smile. "I came looking for you before it got too late, but we better hurry back." Shaking his head, he muttered, "Alpha Stewart is in a snit because that Cayden guy from the wolf pack up north called asking about Jocomo. Alpha's ranting and raving about homos and meddlesome wolves." Frowning, Marc told him, "Be careful tonight. It won't take much to set him off."

"I can't believe he thinks he can get away with kidnapping a shifter from another pack," Taylor muttered, lowering to a crouch as Marc did the same beside him. "He's just asking for trouble."

"Don't let him hear you say that," Marc warned. Then he leaned over and sniffed at him before smirking. "You out here having a little fun?"

Taylor fought back a blush as he shrugged. "Stress relief. Ya know?"

Marc grimaced as he nodded. "I'm sorry you have to hide, man."

"At least he's not trying to force me to breed," Taylor offered with a sympathetic grimace. "Has the alpha set a date for your wedding to Emily, yet?"

Heaving a sigh, Marc shook his head. "No. Jocomo visiting has given him something else to think about, thank the gods," he told him. After a quick glance around, Marc leaned close and whispered, "Maybe this trouble with the wolves will be good for us in the long run."

Taylor knew exactly what Marc was insinuating—having Stewart and Friar removed as their leaders.

"From your lips to God's ears," Taylor whispered back.

Then he shifted.

As Taylor galloped back toward the pack house, he could swear he felt eyes on him, and it warmed his insides just a little.

Chapter Three

Watching Taylor wash off his scent, then head into the woods with a coyote shifter named Marc, was one of the hardest things Ulrick had ever had to do.

Still, he'd understood the necessity of it.

As Taylor had pointed out, if he came up missing or his scent changed due to Ulrick marking him, Ulrick's chance of getting in and out of the territory with as little effort as possible would be next to impossible.

To that end, Ulrick had needed to let his mate go. That didn't stop him from taking to the trees and following his coyote as closely as possible. Ulrick was careful to remain silent and downwind so as not to alert Marc to his presence.

When Ulrick spotted houses between the trees, he slowed. Pausing at the edge of a larger clearing, he crouched in the cover of several branches. Ulrick watched as Taylor and Marc split up, his mate veering to the left toward the largest home.

As Ulrick watched, Taylor paused at the bottom of the deck stairs. He appeared to take a deep breath, as if gathering courage. After a few seconds, Taylor bounded up the stairs and slipped in through the doggie door.

With Taylor out of sight, Ulrick barely fought back a growl of displeasure. He forced himself to rein in his annoyance. Gathering his self-control, Ulrick began sweeping his gaze over the area. Due to the trees interspersed through the area, he knew he couldn't see all the homes, and he tried to recall the map Cayden had provided.

Turning on the branch, Ulrick carefully made his way back

the way he'd come. He rounded the village as much as possible, but he couldn't get close to the home where Jocomo's mother lived. It was too close to the central pack house that Taylor had entered.

Ulrick wondered if those closer to the center were higher-ranking members or held more sway. Considering the pack had been taken over by the trio less than a decade before, it could have just been a coincidence. Either way, Ulrick would need to rethink his strategy.

Time to get my clothes.

Turning away from the village—and Taylor with it—tested Ulrick's self-control. He'd never been so concerned about another that he didn't want to leave him . . . or her. His life had been the military, and he'd never had a relationship.

This mate thing is seriously messing with me.

Even as he mentally grumbled to himself, Ulrick knew he couldn't and wouldn't change it. As he made his way out of coyote territory, he thought of all the mated couples in the Stone Ridge pack. While there had been bumps along the way as they'd bonded, each and every pair had ended up damn near perfect for each other.

While Ulrick had never considered who could be that perfect person for himself, he guessed the Fates had decided for him.

Taylor, a cute, hazel-eyed coyote shifter with dirty-blond hair that Ulrick already found himself longing to touch once more.

So, the faster I get my stuff and return, the faster I can have Taylor in my arms again.

And this time, I'm not stopping until I claim him.

As much as Ulrick had wanted to do just that beside the waterfall, he'd known it was impossible. After all, he hadn't had any lube. While he could be an asshole at times, he would never subject anyone to taking him with just his spit for lube.

I'm not that big an asshole.

With his mind on fucking Taylor, Ulrick made quick work of returning to his stuff. He shifted before retrieving the backpack from the tree. After donning his clothes and boots, Ulrick pulled out a bag of jerky and began munching on a piece as he started back the way he'd come.

What had been a thirty-minute jog in jaguar form took Ulrick nearly two hours on his human feet. He listened closely to everything around him, trusting his jaguar's instincts to give him a heads-up if there was trouble. Ulrick heard noises to his left, and he quickly scurried up a tree.

"I'm telling you, Kris," a deep voice snarled. "I smelled somethin' on that little pipsqueak. Something I didn't recognize."

"Did you ask him what it was, Friar?" A different man answered—maybe Kris.

"Course I did," the first man responded—Friar, evidently. "The bitch had the audacity to lie to me." The man's voice turned cruel. "I taught him, though. Taylor won't be movin' right for a week, at least."

Kris scoffed. "He better still keep up with his chores."

"I didn't bust him up that bad," Friar grumbled. "He'll keep up."

Ulrick felt his gut clench, and he gritted his teeth as he watched a pair of men appear from between the trees. He was so damn tempted to leap on them, letting his jaguar out in the process. He could shred the pair before they knew what hit him. Ulrick could take them out in human form just as easily.

Just a quick wrench of Friar's neck and—

"Where'd you leave Taylor?" Kris asked, his tone mild. "Penny cleaning him up?"

"Naw, I locked him in his rooms at the house," Friar replied with a curl of his lip. "The little shit still didn't tell me what I wanted to know, so he can clean his own backside." Laughing darkly, he added, "He'll probably be pissin' blood for a day or two."

Ulrick dug his fingernails into the bark of the tree, his body practically vibrating with his desire to end the fucker.

"Damn, he still didn't tell you what the scent was?" Kris sounded shocked. "After you beat him bloody?"

"No."

"And you're sure it wasn't someone from the pack?" Kris pressed, their voices growing fainter as they moved further away. "Maybe he was hookin' up with one of the older women that we just haven't gotten around to enjoying yet."

"Could be," Friar conceded. "But I'm goin' to follow his backtrail. See if I can figure it out, just to be sure."

"I'll join you," Kris claimed. "I could do with a run."

Friar grunted in response, and a few seconds later, Ulrick heard the unmistakable snap and pop of shifters changing form. The noises went on for nearly twenty seconds, telling him that one of the pair was a little slow. Ulrick clenched his jaw, barely resisting the renewed urge to take them out.

Instead, Ulrick waited.

If the beta and head enforcer are running in the trees, that means only the alpha and a second enforcer are at the pack house.

Ulrick counted to thirty after the noises ceased. Then he jumped down and began stealthily jogging toward the house. His mate was injured and alone. It was time to go find him.

Working his way a little to the south, Ulrick kept downwind of many of the homes. He paused at the side of a run-down-looking cabin. From the musty scent and the peeling paint, Ulrick knew it wasn't currently occupied.

In the shadows, Ulrick glanced up at the sky. The growing shadows offered him cover, and he easily made use of them. Ulrick crept from one home to a tree and to another home.

Finally, Ulrick stood fifty paces from the largest dwelling. He saw the lights on in several downstairs rooms, as well as a couple of upstairs ones. Ulrick really wished he could circle the place, but he knew that would leave him too exposed.

Wish I'd asked Taylor which room was his.

As if in response to his silent plea, Ulrick spotted movement in the second-story window to the far left of the house. His breath caught in his throat when he spotted Taylor's face and torso. The coyote shifter rested his palm on the glass as his features twisted into a pain-filled expression.

Even then, Ulrick found himself thinking of just how gorgeous his little mate was.

After a quick glance around to confirm that no one was in sight, Ulrick stepped out of the shadows. He knew the second Taylor spotted him. His lover's jaw sagged open, and his eyes widened almost comically. Taylor even appeared to glance around, as much as his position in the window allowed, anyway.

For just an instant, Ulrick wished Taylor was ex-military. Then he would be able to use hand signals to speak to him. Except, Ulrick wouldn't want Taylor's soft edges to be hardened by battle. He truly liked his little lover just the way he was.

Gods, I'm thinking some bizarre shit.

After another glance around, Ulrick jogged across the yard. He quickly flattened himself against the side of the building, directly under Taylor's window. Ulrick stared upward, listening as the wood groaned a little when Taylor managed to open the window just a crack.

"I-I can't open it anymore," Taylor told him, his voice barely a whisper. "I d-don't think I could crawl out anyway."

Even with Taylor's voice so soft, Ulrick could still hear the pain within its depths. His cat snarled in his mind, and he suddenly wished he'd given in to his earlier urge. Ulrick wished he'd snapped that fucking Friar's neck.

Unable to change the past, Ulrick pushed the thought out of his mind. He stared upward as he told Taylor, "It's okay, baby." He did his best to sound soothing. "I heard Friar and Kris talking in the woods. I know what he did to you." Ulrick couldn't quite keep the growl out of his voice, and he hoped his mate didn't think he was upset with him. After all, nothing could have been further from the truth. "How many people are in the house? And do you have any idea where?"

"Why?"

"Because I'm coming in to get you, Taylor," Ulrick declared. "Friar and Kris are heading to the waterfall, so I know they're gone," he added, ignoring Taylor's obvious gasp of shock. "I'd prefer not to run into too many people, so tell me who's here and where, if you can."

For a long moment, Taylor didn't respond.

Ulrick glanced around, barely resisting his desire to urge his mate to hurry up. He didn't particularly care for standing out there, exposed and in the open. Needing his cute coyote to trust him, Ulrick waited.

"Um, well, the cook and her daughter are probably cleaning or prepping for tomorrow's meals in the kitchen," Taylor began slowly, his voice hitching with pain. "A-And Alpha Stewart is probably in his office. Um, that's the second door on the right, facing the front of the house." After another few heartbeats, Taylor told him, "If Friar and Kris are out, then the only others here should be in their rooms already. The alpha likes the house to be quiet when he's in his office at night, unless he calls for one of us because he wants something."

"Do I need to go through the kitchen to get to your room?" Ulrick asked, frustrated that he didn't know the lay of the house.

"N-No," Taylor replied. "The back door, the one with the doggie door in it, opens to a back foyer," he explained quickly. "The servants' stairs are right there."

"Good," Ulrick rumbled. "Now pack a bag, baby. I'll be right up."

After another glance around, Ulrick started around the house. He paused at the corner and peeked around it. Seeing a child playing in the dirt at the back of a nearby house, Ulrick watched the boy for a moment.

Ulrick confirmed that the child was focused on playing with the backhoe toy, using the bucket to dig in one spot and pile the dirt in another one. Keeping to the shadows as much as possible, he strode purposefully to the back door. Ulrick used his peripheral vision to keep an eye on the child, but he knew a running figure would draw more attention than someone walking.

Reaching the door, Ulrick gripped the knob. The door gave easily and swung open on silent hinges. Ulrick stepped into the foyer, quickly closing the door behind him.

Hearing the low tones of two women through the half-open door on his left, Ulrick headed toward the stairs straight ahead. On silent feet, he quickly ascended the steep staircase. Ulrick figured the place had been built before safety regulations were put in place for stair height and angle.

Ulrick reached the top and paused, taking a second to confirm the hallway was empty. Using his nose, he easily figured out which room was Taylor's. After all, the heavy odor of his mate's blood still hung in the air. The iron-rich scent caused Ulrick's mouth to water even as his gut churned with renewed anger at what Beta Friar had done to his mate.

Never again.

When Ulrick gripped the knob, he wasn't surprised to find it locked, considering the beta had mentioned that. He debated what to do—break it or pick it. After a second, Ulrick chose to pick it. That way, if Beta Friar came to check on Taylor at some point, it would take him longer to realize his mate was gone.

Ulrick crouched, pulled a lockpick set from his boot, and got to work.

Chapter Four

Perching on the edge of the wooden chair, Taylor waited as he listened to someone work the lock. He couldn't smell much over the blood still oozing from the lashings on his back. His gut churned with unease even as he prayed that his mate could rescue him.

Taylor watched the door swing open, and his breath caught in his throat. Never had a man's hard features looked so damn good to him. While Taylor would never call Ulrick classically handsome, he wondered what Ulrick's thin slash of a mouth would taste like.

We haven't done that yet. Maybe he doesn't kiss.

"Hi, baby," Ulrick whispered in his deep voice. He smiled just a little before glancing around the room, and the expression slipped from his features. "Damn."

Taylor understood the reaction. The room didn't hold much. There was a metal frame holding a twin-sized mattress, a nightstand beside it, and a desk with the hard chair he was sitting on. At least he had a tiny jack-and-jill bathroom that he shared with Neil, but Beta Friar had put the fear of god into Neil, and the other coyote shifter had locked his door to the bathroom.

Oh well. I really do understand why he did it. No one wants to get on Beta Friar's bad side.

According to the inner circle, Taylor could have more things when he earned them. Of course, there was no way for him to do that because they would never allow him to be more than a servant to them. Before they'd taken over, Taylor had lived in one of the small cottages by himself. They'd confiscated most of his belongings, selling what they could and giving some items to other pack members that they considered more deserving.

That meant those pack members were bigger, stronger, or sucked up to them more.

"Where's your bag, Taylor?"

Taylor blinked and realized that Ulrick was crouching before him. He must have zoned out, probably due to the pain. With a tremulous smile, Taylor pointed. "Tucked in the closet," he whispered. "I don't have much."

Ulrick nodded as he swept his gaze over Taylor's seated form. "I smell the blood," he murmured. His attention snagged on the cut-off sweatshorts that Taylor wore—it was the only thing he was wearing. "I'll clean you up properly once we're away from here. Do you have a change of clothes or two in your bag?"

As Ulrick spoke, he rose to his feet and crossed the room. If Taylor hadn't been staring right at his mate, he wouldn't have even realized the man was in the room. Ulrick seemed to move like a ghost. He was that quiet.

"Yeah," Taylor confirmed as he eased to his feet. His legs stung, uncomfortable at his movements, as Beta Friar had worked over his thighs, too. "A couple of them."

"I have a first aid kit in my backpack," Ulrick revealed as he slung the bag over his shoulder. "But do you have any towels to clean those?" His nostrils flared, and a muscle ticked in his jaw. "Gods, I should have killed that asshole when I had the chance."

Taylor didn't really know what Ulrick was talking about. *What chance?* Instead, he answered his question.

"We could grab a hand towel from the bathroom," Taylor recommended, pointing to the open doorway. "There's salve on the counter, too."

Ulrick nodded once before disappearing into that room. He was back a second later, tucking the jar of salve into the backpack. He'd shoved a hand towel into his back pocket, the end dangling from it to cover some of his ass as he moved past Taylor.

Too bad.

Pausing just past him, Ulrick peered at him over his shoulder. "I'll make certain the coast is clear," he told him. His expression turned uncertain as he said, "Perhaps I should wrap that blanket around you and carry you?"

Nibbling his bottom lip, Taylor tried to fight down his fear at that idea. He understood why Ulrick was offering. Taylor couldn't move very fast with his injuries. Still, he didn't want to imagine how much being carried would hurt, either.

"I-I can keep up," Taylor promised, clenching and unclenching his hands. After a second of hesitation, he added, "And you might end up needing to carry Jocomo."

Taylor couldn't imagine what state the wolf shifter would be in after being Beta Friar's prisoner for a week.

"Shit, right," Ulrick growled. With a shake of his head, he headed to the door. He peeked out, then led the way into the hall. "Start toward the stairs while I relock this."

Doing as he'd been ordered, Taylor limped toward the stairs. By the time he reached the top, Ulrick was right beside him. He peered down the steep steps and bit back a whimper. Taylor knew that bending his legs was going to hurt.

Sucking it up—*after all, this is my chance to get away from this life*—Taylor began his descent. He clenched his teeth to stop himself from crying out from the pain. The tickle of blood oozing down his thighs told him he would be leaving tracks.

"Shit, baby," Ulrick hissed. "I'm so sorry."

Taylor didn't know why Ulrick was apologizing . . . until he felt his big lover sweep him into his arms and rush him down the stairs. Even as he managed to bite back his whimper, he couldn't help the tears that managed to leak from the corners of his eyes.

"Tuck your nose into my neck, Taylor," Ulrick urged, his voice barely more than a whisper. "Breathe in my scent. I've been told shifters find it soothing."

As Taylor obeyed, he was once again reminded that, while Ulrick looked like a shifter, he hadn't started out as one. Taylor wondered how that could possibly be. He'd always been taught that shifters were born, just like vampires, gargoyles, and any other paranormal.

How the hell?

Still, Ulrick's instincts were spot on. As soon as Taylor tucked his nose against the large man's neck and breathed in his scent, it felt as if his pain began to ebb. Maybe that was because his arousal began to soar, but still . . . it was nice.

"That's the way, Taylor," Ulrick murmured, ducking his head to whisper into his ear. "Take a few more deep breaths of my scent, then look up. I need to know where to go to get Jocomo. Is he at his parents' home?"

Taylor obeyed before lifting his head just a little and peering around the area from beneath his lashes. It took him a second to place the trees from his unfamiliar angle.

"Um, we need to go that way." Taylor pointed in a direction, hoping his big strong mate ignored the way his hand trembled a bit. "Around a hundred yards. You'll see an old dead stump. There's a trap door hidden at the base." Taylor's gut clenched just at the idea of heading down into that dark, enclosed space. "It's where they keep . . . those who displease them."

Taylor trembled in Ulrick's hold, unable to help himself. He'd been down there once . . . when the assholes had first taken over the coyote pack. When they'd booted him from his home and instituted their new laws—including taking most of his meager possessions—Taylor had made the mistake of speaking up.

They hadn't been pleased.

A few days chained in that dark, dank hold, undergoing beatings a number of times, had made Taylor learn to bite his tongue. When he'd been pulled from that hellhole, every bisexual male in the place had suddenly been straight as an arrow. Taylor had learned damn fast to be exactly the same.

Even though Taylor was essentially turned into slave labor, he'd been so damn grateful for his small stature. He'd had to watch as—one-by-one—men and women he'd considered friends, friends who had zero interest in each other, had been mated off to each other. Taylor had blessed his small size each and every time that he'd been overlooked.

And Fate has rewarded me for my perseverance. My mate is here . . . rescuing me.

Considering Ulrick had originally been there for Jocomo, Taylor understood that the big man hadn't originally been there to rescue him. That didn't change the facts of life. Their animals had scented each other, recognized each other as fated mates, and now, they were bound together by the gods themselves.

"You still with me, Taylor?" Ulrick asked softly, jostling him ever-so-gently.

Taylor whimpered, but the move allowed him to dredge up a bit of consciousness. He realized he'd been about to pass out, and he knew that wouldn't help either of them. Biting his tongue, Taylor hummed as he nodded a bit.

"Y-Yeah," Taylor managed. Turning his head, he glanced around the area. "There." He waved his hand to indicate the stump drawing closer on his left, considering Ulrick was still moving. "That's the stump."

"Is there a lock?"

Taylor shook his head once. "No," he whispered. "They think the location is a secret."

Ulrick nodded once. "Okay, baby," he murmured, pausing beside the indicated stump. "I'm gonna have to put you down. Do you want to sit or stand?"

Spotting a fallen log, Taylor pointed at it. "There, please."

Doing as Taylor requested, Ulrick gently lowered him to the log.

Taylor perched on it, making certain his legs didn't touch the rough bark. Forcing a smile, he pointed at the stump. Just as he opened his mouth, he spotted the hatch at the base of it start to open, and he gasped, instead.

Ulrich glanced sharply behind him, immediately spotting what Taylor had noticed. Drawing the gun from the holster attached to his thigh, he pointed it at whoever was exiting. The man was halfway up the steps when he lifted his attention from the climb, revealing his features in the darkness.

"Jeremy," Taylor whispered in surprise. "What are you doing here?"

Jeremy's attention glanced at Taylor before his focus riveted on Ulrick and the weapon he held. "Who—Who are you?" Frowning, Jeremy straightened his spine and softly demanded, "What are you doing here? What do you want?"

Instead of answering Jeremy's questions, Ulrick asked, "You're Jeremy?" He glanced back at Taylor. "This is Jocomo's brother? The one he came to visit?"

Taylor nodded. "Yeah." Cocking his head, he returned his attention to Jeremy. "Were you, um, sneaking Jocomo food or something?"

"Yeah," Jeremy replied. "And water and I cleaned up Jocomo's fresh round of cuts."

Ulrick lowered the gun and returned it to his holster. "I'm Ulrick Lanston," he told him, moving toward Jeremy. "I was sent by Alpha Declan to find Jocomo when he disappeared."

"Alpha Declan," Jeremy murmured, eyeing Ulrick warily. "You'll take Jocomo to safety?"

After a nod, Ulrick asked, "If you knew where they were keeping Jocomo, why didn't you report it?" His eyes narrowed as he continued, "Or get him out of there?"

"He's chained up, and I can't open them," Jeremy replied, his shoulders sagging as he lowered his gaze to the ground. "And even if I let him go, I didn't know where to take him. He's unconscious, and I don't know where his pack lands are . . . or even if I'd be accepted there." Lifting his gaze back to Ulrick, Jeremy whispered, "He came here to see me and Mom. What if they blame me for this? I— "

"Hey, they won't blame you." Ulrick settled his hand on Jeremy's shoulder. "You have a car or truck?"

"No." Jeremy glanced at Taylor. "But I know where Dad keeps the keys to his. I can swipe them." Then he frowned. "But the second I start it, one of the inner circle will come running. We're not allowed to leave pack lands without permission."

"Gods, the more I hear about these assholes, the more I want to kill 'em," Ulrick grumbled with a shake of his head.

"You can't," Taylor claimed, worry flooding him.

When Ulrick arched one brow and stated flatly, "I assure you, babe. I could, and I wouldn't lose any sleep over it."

Taylor shook his head swiftly. "No, I mean, I'm sure you could, but if you kill them without challenging them, then you'd be labeled rogue, and you'd be hunted."

"*Babe?*" Jeremy cut in softly, glancing between them, confusion knitting his dark brows.

Ulrick nodded. "We're mates." Then he grumbled, "And I have zero desire to lead a coyote pack, so no way will I challenge them." Scoffing, he added, "Or hell, any pack, for that matter." With that said, Ulrick refocused on Jeremy. "Let's get Jocomo out of here and worry about the getting away part once we reach the truck."

"But I told you," Jeremy countered, frowning. "He's chained up."

"I can fix that," Ulrick assured, pulling Jeremy the last couple of steps out of the tunnel. Turning to face Taylor, he asked,

"You okay here for a few minutes while I get Jocomo?"

Taylor nodded, clenching his fingers together. "Yeah," he murmured, even though he was nervous about letting Ulrick out of his sight. While Taylor knew it was irrational, he couldn't help but fear that if Ulrick went into that hole, he would never see him again. Unable to help himself, Taylor whispered, "P-Please hurry."

"Quick as a flash," Ulrick assured. Then he headed down the tunnel.

Jeremy stared after him, looking just as worried. Then he tipped his head up and sniffed. His brows furrowed as he moved toward Taylor.

"Shit," Jeremy hissed, lifting his hands as if wanting to touch Taylor. "What the hell happened?" A growl entered his tone as he muttered, "Did Ulrick do that to you?"

Taylor quickly shook his head. "No, Beta Friar did when I wouldn't tell him the source of a smell he didn't recognize." With a blush, he still felt a bit of pride as he claimed, "I still had a little of Ulrick's scent on me when I served them dinner, but I'd never betray my mate. No matter what."

"Damn, Taylor," Jeremy murmured. He made as if to pat Taylor on the back, but he must have thought better of it, as he let his hand fall back to his side. "I'm happy for you."

"Thanks," Taylor replied quietly, not even bothering to stop his smile. "I can't wait to get out of here."

"I bet." Jeremy grimaced, crossing his arms over his chest. "Me, too," he admitted. His expression turning pensive, he asked, "You really think Jocomo and Ulrick's pack will let me join?"

"If Ulrick says so, then I believe him." Taylor had to have faith in his mate. Except, then he wondered out loud, "Except, he's a jaguar shifter, so what's he doing with a pack of wolves?"

Jeremy's brows shot up. "A jaguar? No shit?" As Taylor

nodded, nibbling his bottom lip with unease, Jeremy whispered, "Maybe Jocomo will be able to tell us when he wakes up."

Or I'll just ask my mate when we're somewhere safe.

Except, right then, the sound of a coyote's howl rent the air . . . and Taylor thought it was way too close for comfort.

Chapter Five

The hole the inner circle was keeping Jocomo chained up in was exactly that—a hole. Someone had probably expanded an old animal den into a ten-by-ten pit. The dirt walls were damp on two sides. A couple of wooden slats had been pressed into the earth on the front, creating the stairs. The back was dirty stone.

It was there that Ulrick found Jocomo. Two chains had been embedded into the rock around four feet high, affixing Jocomo's wrists in thick manacles. With a length of maybe a foot of chain, it meant he couldn't lie down. There was another pair at ground level and attached to his ankles.

Jocomo hung limply in his restraints. His feet were bare, and he wore only a pair of ragged gym shorts. His dark hair hung lank across his forehead, and his skin gleamed in the scant light that filtered into the hole. The red welts and oozing sores were in various stages of healing, telling Ulrick that Jocomo had been beaten on more than one occasion.

Setting his backpack on the ground, Ulrick quickly pulled out his phone. He took several pictures for evidence, planning to send them to Alpha Declan. After returning the device to his pocket, Ulrick hurried to Jocomo's side.

Ulrick pulled his lockpicks free once more and started working on the manacles. When the cuff popped free of Jocomo's right wrist, Ulrick carefully lowered the limb to the shifter's lap. The move pulled a low moan from the wolf shifter's throat.

"Easy, Jocomo," Ulrick rumbled softly as he began unlocking the man's other wrist. "I'm Ulrick," he told him, just in case the man was actually aware. "Alpha Declan sent me to find you, since I'm technically not part of his pack." Ulrick kept his voice low and soothing. "You may remember me from your work. I know you were a manager at Caribou's until recently." Having never been much for small talk, Ulrick racked his brain for something—anything—to say. "Oh, you remember Earl, one of the servers there?" He didn't bother waiting for an answer as he removed the manacle from Jocomo's second wrist and moved on to one on his ankle. "Well, Earl found his mate. A human named Goliath, and he totally lives up to his name." Now comfortable with the type of lock he was working on, he quickly finished the third and moved on to the last. "He's the new deputy in town, so another guy in law enforcement in Stone Ridge who's in the know about the supernatural. I think Alpha Declan is pretty pleased."

"H-Happy for Earl," Jocomo slurred softly, his voice rough.

As Ulrick removed the last manacle, he noticed Jocomo managing to open his left eyelid a little. The right one was swollen shut.

"Remember." Jocomo coughed, and Ulrick put away his lockpicks and grabbed a bottle of water from his bag. "R-Remember y-you."

Ulrick lifted the bottle to Jocomo's lips and helped him take a small sip. "Glad to hear it, Jocomo." As he assisted the wolf shifter in taking another swallow, the sound of a coyote's yipping call reached his ears. "Shit," Ulrick muttered. "Time to go." Closing the water bottle, he warned, "This is probably going to hurt."

Without waiting for a response, Ulrick shoved the bottle back into his bag, then swung the backpack over his left shoulder. He slid his arms under Jocomo's body. As Ulrick hefted the big man, he felt grateful for his increased shifter strength. Otherwise, he wasn't entirely certain he would have been able to carry the man up the stairs.

While Jocomo groaned softly, he didn't protest the movement.

Jeremy met Ulrick nearly at the top. "Let me take him," he offered, holding out his arms. "You'll need to take your mate."

Ulrick nodded as he handed Jocomo to Jeremy. At the same time, he looked past the pair, searching for his mate. Ulrick's heartrate sped up, and he didn't like the look of terror that was filling Taylor's eyes.

My mate should never look like that, damn it!

Rushing to Taylor's side, Ulrick swept up his mate's bag where he'd left it at the man's feet earlier. "Sorry, baby," he muttered before once again taking Taylor into his arms.

To Ulrick's pleasure, Taylor barely whimpered even as he immediately wrapped his arms around Ulrick's neck. He turned and began jogging after Jeremy. Ulrick mentally kept his fingers crossed that the other shifter was taking them to the truck he'd mentioned.

"Shit, that's my mother on the porch," Jeremy warned, skidding to a stop next to the truck parked in front of a cottage.

"Will she try to stop us?" Ulrick asked, taking in the tired lines and sadness around the woman's eyes and lips.

"I don't know," Jeremy admitted as he yanked open the passenger side door. He shoved an unconscious Jocomo inside, pushing him to the middle of the bench seat. Then Jeremy turned and began heading toward the porch. "Mom, I—"

Jeremy didn't get any further before she tossed a set of keys toward him. The shifter caught them easily, his expression questioning.

Without a word, his mother turned and headed back into

the house.

"Well, that answers that," Ulrick muttered, settling Taylor onto the seat next to Jocomo. "Get in and drive, Jeremy," Ulrick ordered, closing the door.

Frowning at him even as he slid behind the wheel, Jeremy asked, "What are you doing?"

"Providing cover," Ulrick replied before deftly bounding into the bed of the old pick-up. With one knee on the metal bed, he propped the boot of his other leg against the wheel well, bracing himself. Pulling his *Glock*, Ulrick hollered, "Drive."

Jeremy fired up the pick-up, the engine turning over easily, just as a big coyote came barreling from between the trees. That one was followed swiftly by a slightly smaller animal. A second later, the front door of the main house slammed open, revealing a large, clearly angry man.

"Stop them!" the guy yelled.

Ulrick took aim at the man who had to be Alpha Stewart. With the jostling of the truck, he aimed a little wide and to the right. He didn't want to actually hit the asshole, after all. Taking Taylor's warning to heart, Ulrick had no desire to take the chance of being labeled rogue.

The round slammed into the porch railing, causing Alpha Stewart to duck and flinch. A second later, he disappeared back into the house.

Coward.

Smirking, Ulrick aimed at the closer of the two coyotes. He squeezed off a shot, hitting the dirt to the large beast's right. The animal snarled but kept coming. Ulrich saw several more of the shifters coming at them from the left.

"Speed up, Jeremy," Ulrick ordered. "I don't want to actually hit any of these assholes." Then he grinned as he felt the truck lurch faster. "Which of the pair back there is Friar?"

Maybe I want to hit one after all.

"Uh, the grayer one," Jeremy replied. "Tight turn ahead.

Hang on!"

Obviously anticipating the turn, the pair of coyotes joined the trio and ducked into the woods. Ulrick figured the group was trying to head them off. Maybe they thought Jeremy would veer to avoid them if they were on the road.

Hell, they're probably right about that.

Adjusting his position, Ulrick gripped the side of the bed. When Jeremy barreled around the curve, his knee slipped, and he almost went down. With a flex of his thigh, he managed to keep himself upright just in time to see the coyotes burst from the trees.

Just as Ulrick had surmised, the group—led by Friar and probably Kris—veered toward the road a little ways in front of Jeremy. With a sneer, Ulrick leveled his *Glock*. He steadied his arm as he blew out a slow breath, then squeezed the trigger.

Ulrick watched as Friar yipped and dropped, the shifter's body sliding across the ground from the momentum of the bullet hitting him. The other coyotes scattered, giving Jeremy time to fly past them. Eyeing the group, Ulrick could see their indecision. The beasts looked at the fallen beta, the enforcer who was sniffing at Friar, and the retreating truck.

As much as it galled Ulrick, he felt a measure of relief when Friar's head popped up before he staggered to three of his paws. He held his left rear leg off the ground, and Ulrick could see the dribble of blood, telling him that he'd hit Friar right where he'd been aiming—his lower haunch. The asshole would live.

A second later, Ulrick heard the roar of an engine that wasn't their old stolen truck. A large SUV appeared behind them, skidding around the turn in the road. For a second, Ulrick thought perhaps the vehicle would stop to help Friar. Then it flew past the pack of coyotes, barreling toward them.

"Son of a bitch," Ulrick snarled, readying his *Glock* once more.

The vehicle was in much better repair than the old truck Jeremy was driving, and Ulrick knew that it wouldn't be long before it overtook them. He narrowed his eyes and checked the cab. The driver was an angry-faced Alpha Stewart. Someone Ulrick didn't know was in the passenger seat, but the fact that he was readying a revolver of some kind told him enough.

Hmmm . . . where to hit him.

Ulrick went with the obvious—the tires. It took two shots, but he managed it. The right front tire exploded, and the SUV went careening off the road. Spraying dirt and gravel into the air, Alpha Stewart managed to slide the vehicle to a stop just before hitting a tree.

Grinning widely, Ulrick watched the alpha jump from the SUV. He saw the man shake his fist in their direction. Chuckling darkly, Ulrick lifted his left hand and flipped the alpha the bird.

A second later, a shot rang out, and their taillight exploded.

Right, the other asshole has a gun.

Ulrick ducked behind the tailgate as another shot made the metal ding loudly.

Fortunately, after that, Jeremy turned another corner, and the pair, as well as the disabled SUV, disappeared from sight.

Relaxing a little, Ulrick reholstered his *Glock*. He turned to peer through the pick-up's rear window. Ulrick saw that, at some point, both Jocomo and Taylor had crouched as low as they could in the cab. Even Jeremy was slouched so much Ulrick wasn't entirely certain how the shifter managed to see the road.

When Taylor peered up at him with wide hazel eyes filled with fear, Ulrick gave his mate an encouraging smile and a thumbs up.

Taylor's look of relief, as well as the small, tremulous smile that curved his full lips, sent a completely inappropriate wash of desire through Ulrick.

Oh well. It's a mate thing.

Jeremy glanced at Ulrick in the rearview mirror. Reaching back, he opened the middle sliding window.

"We okay?" Jeremy asked. "You okay?"

"I'm fine," Ulrick assured. "And as long as those last few shots didn't hit anything vital on the truck, we're all good."

Jeremy sighed deeply, his shoulders slumping even as he straightened in his seat. "Where to, then?" he asked after a glance at Jocomo. "To Jocomo's wolf pack?"

Ulrick hesitated an instant before answering, "Not straight away." Seeing Jeremy's brows crease, he explained, "I need to talk to Alpha Declan first. Get shifter procedure for this."

No way did Ulrick want to land a mess in Alpha Declan's lap if anything he'd done went against shifter protocols.

"Plus, that's a long ass drive," Ulrick added, pulling out his phone. He pulled up his maps app to check towns within a forty-mile radius. "Let's head east. Your pack won't expect it," he offered, guessing Alpha Stewart would assume that he was heading straight to Stone Ridge. "We'll get a couple of hotel suites, clean up Jocomo and Taylor, and get some food in everyone."

Jeremy winced before admitting, "I don't have any money."

"Neither do I," Taylor whispered, hunching his shoulders.

"Don't even worry about it. I got this."

One nice thing about working with the Stone Ridge wolves was that they had plenty of resources, and that included the funds to care for whoever they considered their own.

And oddly enough, that's me now.

Chapter Six

Watching Ulrick stride through the hotel doors, Taylor felt a fissure of unease flood him. He couldn't help but glance out the windows. Between the scent of his blood, Jocomo's blood, as well the stink of his fear, Taylor couldn't get himself to settle.

Only having Ulrick in sight seemed to calm Taylor.

Wow, these mating urges are weird.

"Just try to relax, Taylor," Jeremy murmured, even as he glanced around, too. "We'll be okay."

Considering the uneasy scent pouring off the larger coyote shifter, Taylor wasn't entirely certain the man believed his own words.

Taylor understood why they had to wait in the truck. After all, he was only wearing shorts and a pair of battered sneakers, and his body was covered in lash marks. Jocomo was in a worse state than himself.

While Jeremy could have headed in with Ulrick, there was no reason for him to. Plus, the man really didn't want to leave his brother. Taylor understood that.

So they sat in the truck and waited . . . for what felt like forever, even though, according to the clock in the dash, it'd only been seven minutes.

Seeing Ulrick approaching the sliding glass doors, Taylor let out a relieved sigh. He watched his mate exit the building and jog to the truck. With a quick jump, Ulrick was back in the bed, and Jeremy opened the window again.

"Drive around the building to the right," Ulrick ordered. "I got us a two-bedroom suite on the top floor around back. The truck will be out of sight, and there's a separate entrance, so no one will see Taylor and Jocomo."

Jeremy nodded and started the vehicle moving. Once he'd parked where indicated, he turned off the truck.

"Let's get you guys upstairs," Ulrick rumbled, dropping from the bed once more. "Get you comfortable."

"Okay," Taylor whispered, glancing around the parking area again, but everything appeared quiet. As he took in the height of the building, he wondered, "Why the top floor?"

Taylor couldn't help but think that would make escaping difficult if Alpha Stewart somehow tracked them there.

"Because they didn't have any suites on the ground floor, and I wanted you comfortable." Ulrick shrugged as he cleared his throat. "Sorta wanted to pamper you."

Upon smelling the hint of embarrassment in Ulrick's scent, Taylor smiled shyly up at him. "Thank you."

Ulrick smiled back.

Reaching the door, Ulrick held a key card up to a reader, and the light on the box changed from red to green. He opened the door and held it for Taylor, as well as Jeremy, who was carrying Jocomo. Once inside the foyer, Ulrick paused and glanced around.

There were stairs to the left and a hallway straight ahead.

"Uh, the elevator is that way." Ulrick used his chin to indicate the hallway. His attention strayed to the stairs, betraying his preference. "But we have a better chance of staying out of sight by taking the stairs."

Jeremy shrugged. "My brother's still unconscious." His gaze fell on Taylor. "Up to you, man." He winced. "Those look like they'll hurt."

With a sigh, Taylor nodded. "Stairs are fine. I can handle it."

"Would it be easier if I carried you again?" Ulrick asked

softly, using a hand on the back of Taylor's neck to guide him toward the stairs.

As Jeremy started up the stairs, Taylor eyed them. He nibbled his bottom lip as he met Ulrick's gaze. "I don't want you thinking I'm weak," he admitted.

"You took a thrashing, baby," Ulrick replied, his dark eyes peering at him intensely. "I don't think you're weak." Sliding the backs of his forefingers along Taylor's jaw, Ulrick added, "And just because I wasn't born a shifter doesn't mean I don't have the instinct to take care of you, same as any shifter." Then his expression turned wry as he admitted, "And I've never been in a relationship, never even thought about it, so I'm bound to screw up a time or two as we figure ourselves out."

"Never been in a relationship, either," Taylor admitted, nuzzling into Ulrick's fingers as he peered at him through his lashes. "We'll get there." Then, because he knew it would be easier and faster, Taylor murmured, "And if you don't mind carrying me, I'd appreciate it."

Ulrick smiled again, the move even bigger than the last one. "Okay. Hang on tight, baby."

In the next instant, Taylor once again found himself swept into Ulrick's arms. He bit his bottom lip, doing his best to ignore the pain caused by his mate's fabric-covered arms pressing into the sores on his back. At least with Ulrick's other arm under his knees, he wasn't touching any on his thighs. That didn't stop his own shorts from having rubbed at them, especially on the drive away from the pack. Taylor knew he'd reopened many of the wounds.

Ulrick took the stairs swiftly, doing an impressive job of holding Taylor steady so as not to jostle him.

When they reached the fifth-floor landing, Jeremy was waiting there for them. He still carried Jocomo, although he was leaning with his back against the wall.

Jeremy's smile appeared a little strained as he pushed off the wall. "Everything okay?"

"Yeah. Sorry to keep you waiting," Ulrick stated as he eased Taylor back to his feet. "Come on."

Ulrick led the way to a door with a five-zero-one on the plaque next to it. "This is a two-bedroom suite," he told them, using the card to open the door and lead the way inside. "So we're near each other for safety."

Jeremy nodded, his expression showing how impressed he was as he peered around the central sitting room. "Damn," he whispered. "This is . . . really nice."

Taylor completely agreed. The black sofa appeared plush and cushy, the TV on the wall the couch faced was huge, and there was a decent-sized kitchenette and dining room table near the back. The windows beyond the table, at the back of the room, showed the parking lot abutting to businesses of different sorts.

"Does it matter which bedroom?" Jeremy asked, turning to the right.

Ulrick shook his head. "No," he replied. "From what I understand, both are set up as mirror images with a king-sized bed and bath with both a shower and a tub."

Jeremy nodded and headed to a partially opened door. The corner of a bed could be seen inside the room, and he used his shoulder to push the door the rest of the way open. Then he carefully maneuvered into the room.

Even with his hand firmly on Taylor's neck, Ulrick asked, "Are you going to be okay cleaning Jocomo up by yourself?"

Taylor fought back his growl as the idea of Ulrick seeing a naked Jocomo—even one unconscious and obviously injured—popped into his head.

Jeremy hesitated a few seconds, glancing between them. Then he smirked at Ulrick. "I can handle it," he assured. Arching one brow, he pointed out, "And I don't think Taylor would appreciate that until you're well and truly bonded, man."

Ulrick's black brows shot up, and he snapped his attention to Taylor.

Doing his best to hide his blush, Taylor mumbled, "He's not wrong."

Nodding once, Ulrick began guiding Taylor in the opposite direction. "Right. Forgot about that," he admitted. A bit louder, he called, "I'll leave a number of bandages and ointment on the coffee table out here," he told him. "Even needing to bandage Taylor's wounds, I should have enough for both of us."

"Thanks," Jeremy called before his footsteps thumped as if on bathroom tile.

"Let me spread out the supplies, and I'll be right behind you," Ulrick told Taylor, releasing him in favor of swinging both backpacks off his shoulders. "Do you want to take your stuff into the room?"

"Uh, yeah." Taylor reached out and took his bag. "Thanks."

Even though his satchel was extremely light, the pressure on his arm still pulled at his sensitive back, and he couldn't help but wince.

"Ah, shit. I'm sorry, Taylor." Ulrick quickly took the bag back again. "I'll bring it to you in a minute." He swept his gaze over Taylor's body as he murmured, "If you don't mind, I'd love to wash your back."

Taylor sucked in a sharp breath, and he felt his eyes widen. "O-Okay."

Ulrick placed both bags on the coffee table before focusing on his own. He pulled out a multitude of plastic bags, some holding food and others holding bandages, and others holding tubes and cream.

With Ulrick focused on his task, Taylor headed into the

room that they were evidently going to share. He peered around with interest, taking in the medium blue comforter that he was afraid to touch for fear of getting blood on it. He hurried across the plush carpet, so he could reach the tile of the bathroom floor.

Taylor paused just inside the door and silently mouthed, wow. The bathroom lived up to the main room's promise. As Ulrick had stated, there was a big jetted tub. Under other circumstances, Taylor would have loved to enjoy that. With his torn-up back and thighs, he figured he would be long gone before he was healed enough to try it out.

Bummer.

Fortunately, the large tile shower was just as nice-looking. It was also large enough to fit four men Ulrick's size. He felt dwarfed by it as he opened the door and began messing with the knobs, trying to figure out how it worked.

After a bit of fiddling, Taylor found a soothing temperature. He closed the door to give it a chance to build up some steam. Taylor hesitated a few seconds before he carefully removed his shorts. Seeing all the blood soaked into the back of the legs, he winced.

There's no saving them.

Still, Taylor folded them and placed them on the counter. He would need to ask Ulrick about a safe way of disposing of them. Taylor knew he couldn't just leave them in the trash, as that would run the risk of his blood falling into the wrong hands.

Even his backwater coyote pack knew how dangerous that could be.

Taylor slipped into the shower. He was careful to keep his front to the water to start with, allowing it to hit his feet. Slowly, he eased forward a little at a time, suddenly grateful for the huge size.

When the water hit his thighs, some of it trickled around Taylor's flesh and into his wounds. He hissed softly, pausing.

After a couple of deep breaths, his body accepted the wet heat, and he was able to move forward again.

While Taylor had no idea how long it actually took him to get most of his body under the water, he eventually managed it. Resting his weight on one arm, he stood there, enjoying the heat and exquisite water pressure. It felt so much better than the shower in the bathroom he'd shared.

Hearing the glass door open, Taylor opened his eyes . . . and nearly swallowed his tongue. While he'd felt Ulrick's thickly muscled and heavy frame pressed against him near the waterfall, he hadn't had a chance to really see too much of it. As Ulrick stepped into the shower with him, Taylor looked his fill . . . and there was a *lot* to see.

Ulrick's olive-toned skin seemed to go on for miles. His shoulders were broad with a barrel chest that tapered to a trim, six-pack-covered waist. The muscles on his arms and legs bulged, but not so obscenely as to make one think that he was a bodybuilder. They were deliciously in line with his body.

Taylor found his focus snagged on Ulrick's scars. He had a long thin line along the left side of his lower ribcage that he could imagine was made by a knife. There was a second bit of puckered flesh on the outside of his right thigh. The ridged line reminded Taylor of a repeated belt lash in the same spot over and over again, but he figured that couldn't be the case.

Recalling how Ulrick moved, as well as his precision with the gun he'd had strapped to his thigh, he realized it had to be a bullet wound.

Damn. What has my mate been through? Was he a soldier? How was he made into a jaguar shifter? And to still show compassion to me?

Taylor realized he knew absolutely nothing about the man who'd just slipped into the shower with him. While that did worry him a little, the scent the male gave off soothed him, too. As Taylor watched Ulrick grab a washcloth and soak it, followed by dousing it with soap from a dispenser in the tile wall, he found himself confused about what to say or do.

If he wasn't a shifter, would he have given two shits about me?

Then again, maybe that's how humans feel when a shifter springs the big reveal on them. If it weren't for the mate scent, the instinctual need to bond, would most of us bother taking a second look at that particular human?

In truth, Taylor didn't know, and he couldn't fathom who he could contact to ask.

And it's probably far too late for that, anyway.

"Easy, Taylor," Ulrick rumbled, as if he knew exactly what kinds of thoughts were rattling around in his head. "I may be new to this whole shifter thing, but I've had some great examples." The big man eased closer to him as he massaged the washcloth between his fingers, creating suds. "I'll answer anything you want to know." Scoffing softly, Ulrick gently rested the cloth on Taylor's left shoulder, mostly away from the spray. "Just know that I've had some great men teaching me to understand and communicate with my cat." Resting his other hand on Taylor's bare hip, he lowered his head and crooned just over the sound of the running water, "And my cat wants you so badly, but I won't do a damn thing until your wounds are healed enough so I won't hurt you."

"You won't?" Taylor turned his head away from the water, peering over his shoulder at him. "Why?"

Even to Taylor's own ears, he sounded . . . petulant . . . disappointed.

To Taylor's relief, Ulrick grinned broadly, tipped his head back a little, and laughed. His black eyes appeared to twinkle in the misty spray of the shower. His straight white teeth flashed, and a fond look entered his expression.

"Ah, my pretty coyote shifter." Ulrick winked, his grin turning roguish. "You flatter me." Then he sobered slightly. Although he still swept a hungry gaze over Taylor's naked body. "Don't get me wrong. I want you, and my jaguar wants you. If you weren't injured, I would be all over you like a starving man on a sixty-ounce steak with a bucket of barbeque sauce." Then Ulrick began massaging the soapy cloth over his neck. "And while I can be an asshole at times, I'm not that big an asshole." Lowering his head, Ulrick pecked a kiss to the side of his head before lowering his voice to a husky rumble and saying, "When you're healthy enough to where I don't run the risk of tearing open your welts, I will pound your ass and give you a mating bite so deep, no one will *ever* mistake who you belong to."

A hard shudder worked through Taylor, and even through the pain, he felt his prick stir. Looking over his shoulder, he couldn't help but ask, "Can I give you a claiming scar, too?"

Taylor found himself holding his breath as he waited for a response. He knew some dominant shifters refused to be marked. In his mind, he prayed to the gods that Ulrick wouldn't be like that.

To Taylor's relief, Ulrick grinned broadly as he winked at him. "I can't wait to feel your teeth sink deep into my flesh." With an eyebrow waggle, he added, "I hear it's orgasmic."

As Ulrick began ever-so-gently—and carefully—cleaning his cuts, even the pain couldn't diminish his anticipation.

Gods, I hope I heal fast.

Chapter Seven

Even washing the dirt, debris, bits of fabric, and blood from Taylor's body didn't stop Ulrick from boning up. He did his best to ignore it, however. Ulrick would have thought the occasional soft hisses or flinches should have killed it, but Taylor just smelled way too damn good.

Crouching on the tile floor of the shower, Ulrick carefully finished cleaning up the apparent belt stripes on Taylor's thighs. The fabric of his lover's shorts had rubbed the top ones, and the red, irritated skin began to ooze as soon as he touched them. Ulrick heard Taylor's hiss, and he grimaced, hating that he was causing his pretty shifter pain.

"Almost done," Ulrick murmured, doing his best to soothe his lover. He skimmed the palm of his free hand up and down Taylor's opposite hip, enjoying the feel of the firm flesh. "Then I'll get some ointment and bandages on these." After a second of hesitation, Ulrick added, "I'll get you food, too. Do you have any preferences?"

Ulrick realized there was still so much he needed to learn about the man he would be spending the rest of his life with.

There's plenty of time, though.

"Mmmm, anything is fine," Taylor responded softly, pressing into Ulrick's soothing palm. "I'm not picky."

"Okay." Deciding Taylor could definitely do with some protein to aid in his healing, Ulrick vowed to find something nutritious for him . . . soon. "I'll see what's around here."

"Y-You're leaving?"

Hearing the squeak in Taylor's voice and scenting his fear,

Ulrick quickly reassured the other man. "No, babe." Having done the best he could on the cuts, Ulrick quickly rose to his feet. He dropped the slightly red-stained washcloth onto the floor and reached for Taylor's upper arm. As Ulrick turned the smaller man to face him, he told him, "I'm sure there must be room service or someplace near here that will deliver." Seeing the fear leaving Taylor's eyes, Ulrick rested his hand on each shoulder and gently kneaded the flesh there. His mouth watered with his desire to taste the other shifter, to mark him as his own. Still, Ulrick forced himself to meet Taylor's beautiful hazel eyes and tell him, "It's why I chose a slightly bigger city like this one."

Taylor nodded. "Okay." His smile appeared a little rueful as he added, "Sorry to seem so . . ." His words trailed away, and he finished with a shrug.

"It's okay, babe," Ulrick countered. "This is a huge change for you." Seeing the way Taylor's brows furrowed a little, he quickly amended, "For both of us, actually."

Sliding one hand up, Ulrick cupped Taylor's jaw. While he'd never kissed a man before—hell, he barely bothered to kiss the women he'd bedded in the past—he couldn't deny his desire. In truth, Ulrick didn't want to either.

Ulrick dipped his head and pressed his lips to Taylor's. His intention wasn't to incite, but to soothe. He wanted to connect with his injured mate, but he knew they couldn't do a whole lot right then.

When Taylor pressed forward, Ulrick hummed appreciatively. He eased his palm around to cradle the smaller man's nape. At the same time, he nipped at Taylor's lower lip, requesting entrance.

Taylor instantly opened to him, and Ulrick licked his way into his mouth. He grunted in pleasure as his lover's masculine flavor exploded across his tongue. As Ulrick swallowed Taylor's low moan, he realized he would become addicted to kissing the other man very quickly.

As it should be.

Ulrick eased the kiss to an end and smiled at his panting lover. Taylor's chest heaved against his own, and he felt gratified that the smaller man had enjoyed his kiss just as much. Then Ulrick registered the evidence of how much Taylor had enjoyed it.

Grinning, Ulrick spread his legs as he leaned back against the water-warmed tile wall. Once he was low enough to align their hard cocks, he reached between their bodies and gripped them both in his hand. Ulrick heard Taylor groan, the noise nearly drowned out by the fall of water, as well as Ulrick's own grunt of pleasure.

As Ulrick began to jack them both, he knew it wouldn't take long. He couldn't recall the last time he'd been aroused for so long, and his balls were already pulling tight. His gut churned with the heat of his need, and as he stared into Taylor's heavy-lidded eyes, his heart thudded wildly in his chest.

Taylor sucked in a sharp gasp, and his eyes widened. His body jolted against Ulrick's own. In the next instant, his seed spurted over his hand as a moan of pleasure filled the shower.

"Beautiful," Ulrick managed to growl before his own release hit him.

Roaring his completion, Ulrick jerked as his testicles unloaded. Bliss surged through him in heady waves as he painted Taylor's chest with his seed. Trembles racked him at the intensity of it, and his legs trembled.

If Ulrick hadn't already been leaning on the wall, he feared he would have dropped.

"Wow, baby," Ulrick murmured, smiling down at Taylor. "Just amazing."

"Yeah." With a sigh, Taylor rested his weight against Ulrick. Peering up at him through his lashes, his face flushed and expression sated, he muttered, "Can't wait for you to fuck me."

"Me, too, baby," Ulrick admitted, dropping a kiss to Taylor's oh-so-tempting lips. "Me, too."

Even though releasing Taylor was the last thing Ulrick wanted to do, he knew he needed to get them out of the shower. He had ointment for the welts and open, irritated skin. Plus, Ulrick wanted to get his freshly relaxed mate somewhere comfortable.

After a quick wipe-down, Ulrick turned off the water. He opened the door and grabbed a towel. Ulrick rubbed the soft fabric over Taylor's front before turning him and ever-so-gently dabbing over his back, doing his best to avoid his wounds.

Once done, Ulrick grabbed another towel and wrapped it around his own waist for later. He guided Taylor out of the bathroom. When he pulled the comforter down and urged Taylor to lie on the bed, his mate balked.

"What's wrong?" Ulrick asked in confusion.

Taylor grimaced. "I don't want to get blood on these nice sheets."

Scoffing, Ulrick waggled his brows. "In a day or so, once your wounds are closed, I intend to get something other than blood on these." When he saw Taylor's nostrils flare and scented his cute coyote's renewed arousal, Ulrick chuckled softly. "Here." He dragged the mostly dry towel from his hips and spread it over the bed. "How about that?"

Taylor nodded before carefully climbing on the bed. Lying on his stomach, he let out a long sigh. Peering over his shoulder at him, Taylor smiled at him.

"This is really comfortable," Taylor told him.

"I'm glad," Ulrick replied, thinking that just about *any* bed would have been more comfortable than the small twin in Taylor's room. He didn't mention that, though. Instead, Ulrick headed to the nightstand and grabbed a jar of ointment. "I'm going to put some of this on your welts. It'll soothe the irritation and help you heal faster."

"Okay," Taylor replied.

The trust gleaming in Taylor's hazel eyes caused something to flutter in Ulrick's belly. He did his best to ignore it, already suspecting what it was. Ulrick had heard from other shifters that once they met their fated mate, they fell in lust immediately and love shortly after. Because he wasn't born a shifter, he hadn't expected it to happen to him like that. Still, from the sensations filling Ulrick, he figured he'd been wrong.

I'll already do damn near anything for this man.

Once Ulrick was finished, he screwed the lid back on the jar and placed it on the nightstand. He refocused on Taylor and smiled. His coyote shifter had his eyes closed, and his breathing came in long, relaxed breaths.

Pleased, Ulrick headed back to the bathroom. After drying himself off properly, he pulled on a fresh pair of jeans. While he grabbed a shirt, he didn't pull it on. Instead, he grabbed a pair of gym shorts, too, then headed out to the main room.

After leaving the clothes on the back of the sofa—he figured Jeremy or Jocomo would use them—Ulrick crossed to the mini-fridge. He pulled out a bottle of water and opened it. Once he'd downed half the contents, he closed the bottle and left it on the counter before grabbing another and taking it into the bedroom. Ulrick left that on the nightstand before returning to the main room to explore.

Ulrick found the phone and, as expected, a binder rested next to it. Opening it, he spotted the usual welcome letter. Turning the page, Ulrick read over the room service menu. There were a few things listed that made his stomach growl. Then Ulrick spotted the time and realized the kitchen was closed.

Mentally cursing, Ulrick found a list of local restaurants on the next page. He pulled out his phone and began checking their hours of operation. To Ulrick's relief, there was an all-night diner, as well as a pizza place.

Ulrick headed to the second bedroom and softly rapped on

the slightly ajar door with a knuckle. "Jeremy?" he called softly.

"Come in," Jeremy responded quietly.

Pushing the door partway open, Ulrick slipped inside. He took in the scene at a glance. A cleaned and nude Jocomo lay on the bed. His face was turned toward the door, and the wolf shifter eyed him with his one good eye.

"Hey, Ulrick," Jocomo murmured. A pained smile curved his lips. "Thanks for comin' to get me."

"Happy to help," Ulrick told him. He swept his gaze over the welts and cuts marring his back and thighs, similar to Taylor's, but obviously older. "Wish I'd gotten to you sooner."

With a pained hiss, Jocomo sort of rolled one shoulder. "I'll heal."

"Stop moving," Jeremy ordered from where he stood beside the bed, still putting salve on the wounds on Jocomo's right leg. "Damn that Friar," the coyote shifter snarled. Frowning, he glanced Ulrick's way before returning to his work. "How do we make the bastard pay?"

"I'm going to call Alpha Declan shortly," Ulrick told Jeremy. "He'll know what to do." The alpha wolf seemed to have a lot of connections. "We have two options for dinner," he told them, returning to his initial reason for interrupting them. "There's an all-night diner that does *to go* orders, but I'd need you to pick it up, Jeremy." Seeing Jeremy arch a brow in silent question, Ulrick revealed, "I promised Taylor that I wouldn't leave him. The other option is pizza, and they'll deliver to the hotel, so you'll just have to zip to the lobby to get it."

"I'm okay either way," Jeremy revealed, screwing the lid back on the tub of ointment. Obviously not caring about getting anything on the sheets, he pulled the top one up to cover Jocomo's nudity. "What do you want, bro?"

"If you don't mind going to the diner, I'd kill for a steak,"

Jocomo revealed, eyeing Ulrick. "Do they have steak?"

Nodding, Ulrick pulled the place's menu up on his phone. "They do." He leaned toward Jocomo and showed him the possible sides. "What do you want with it?"

"Mmmm, mashed potatoes, mac and cheese, and a side salad," Jocomo told him without moving.

"Got it." Ulrick handed his phone to Jeremy so he could choose what he wanted. "Stay still and rest. Moving to eat's going to be a bitch." Then Ulrick snapped his fingers. "Oh, damn. I forgot the painkillers."

"Painkillers don't work on shifters," Jeremy murmured absently, even as Ulrick headed out of the room. His attention was obviously still on the menu.

"These do," Ulrick countered, getting them from the items he'd left on the coffee table. It was obvious the man hadn't realized what they were, since he hadn't taken them. "Lark, Alpha Declan's mate, is a doctor, and he and a scientist buddy cooked them up for us," he explained, grabbing a bottle of water from the fridge before returning to the room. "I gotta remember to give one to Taylor when he wakes up."

With a grunt of pain, Jocomo took the pill and popped it into his mouth. He hissed as he arched his back enough to accept several swallows of water. With a sigh, Jocomo rested back on the bed.

"How fast do they work?" Jeremy asked curiously, his concern for his brother obvious. "And I'll have the Cobb salad along with all the fixin's with ranch dressing. Do you mind if I get a slice of blueberry pie for dessert?"

"Mmmm, pie," Jocomo muttered. "Me, too, please."

Ulrick chuckled. "I'll see if we can buy a whole blueberry pie," he told them, thinking that sounded good. "Any idea what Taylor might like?"

Jeremy shrugged. "Sorry. I don't actually know him all that well," he admitted. "But I imagine anything with meat." With a shake of his head, Jeremy explained, "He's been pretty deprived of most things for the last few years."

Nodding once, Ulrick muttered, "Ever since the three stooges took over."

"Right." Jeremy sighed, sitting on the bed beside Jocomo. "I should have warned you away, Jocomo. I'm sorry about this."

"I still would have come, Jeremy," Jocomo told him. "I just woulda been more careful about what I said and to who."

Ulrick could see Jeremy still felt guilty, and he left the brothers to talk, saying that he would order the food. Doing as he'd said, he called the diner and placed their orders, getting two bacon cheeseburgers for himself and Taylor. With one, he got the fries, and with the second, he requested the onion rings. Ulrick appreciated that they sold whole pies.

Heading into his own room, Ulrick checked on Taylor, but his lover still slept. He placed the pain pill next to the water bottle he'd left earlier, hoping he would notice it and take it. Ulrick paused and watched Taylor sleep for a moment, ignoring the way his mind reeled at the sudden changes in his life.

With a sigh, Ulrick reached out and tucked a damp strand of dirty-blond hair behind Taylor's ear. He smiled upon hearing his coyote shifter's hum. The man didn't wake, however, so Ulrick headed back out of the room, leaving the door open so he could hear if Taylor stirred.

Ulrick returned to the brothers' room and told Jeremy when the food would be ready. Then he inhaled deeply before letting it out through pursed lips. Giving the pair a feral smile, Ulrick told them, "Time to call Alpha Declan."

Jocomo returned his hard smile. "He's so gonna bring the pain to those assholes."

"Hell, yeah," Ulrick agreed gruffly.

Chapter Eight

The soft hum of voices filtered into Taylor's mind, pulling him awake. He blinked open his eyes to discover someone—probably Ulrick—had pulled the sheet over him. Evidently, the man had been telling the truth when he'd told him that he didn't care if they got stuff on the sheets.

While Taylor didn't immediately see Ulrick, he could hear his voice, telling him that he was in the next room. The scent of food teased his nostrils, and his stomach grumbled . . . loudly. Taylor realized he hadn't eaten since the noon meal of the prior day, and while the curtains were drawn, he could still see that it was dark out.

Plus, the clock on the nightstand read two-twenty-three AM.

When Taylor's stomach rumbled again, he slowly pushed up with his arms. The sheet stuck to his back a little, adding to the pain of moving. Wincing, Taylor quickly pushed the fabric away before slithering off the side of the bed.

Taylor kept his hands on the mattress as he found his feet. He paused a minute, assimilating the pain while making certain his legs would hold him. Once he felt confident he wouldn't crash to the floor, Taylor straightened away from the bed.

With his vision spinning a little, Taylor took several slow deep breaths. Fortunately, it cleared swiftly enough. He noticed the water bottle on the nightstand and picked it up. As Taylor opened it, he eyed the small round pill there, too, wondering what it was.

After taking several deep swallows, Taylor closed the water and placed it back on the nightstand. He turned, searching for his bag. Spotting it on the dresser, he crossed to it and pulled out a pair of shorts. While all of Taylor's clothes were old and faded, they were clean.

Taylor bent carefully and pulled them on. He hissed when the fabric slid over the welts on his thighs. With a resigned sigh, he returned to the water bottle. Taylor had just picked it up when the door swung wider, and Ulrick stood in the doorway.

"Hi, babe," Ulrick greeted with a smile. "Enjoy your nap?"

Nodding, Taylor admitted, "I think the smell of the food woke me up." His stomach took that second to rumble loud enough that it caused Ulrick to chuckle. "Guess I'm a little hungry."

Ulrick tipped his chin toward the nightstand. "Take your pill, then join us," he encouraged. "I bought you a bacon cheeseburger. There's fries or onion rings," Ulrick added, taking a step backward. "Whichever you prefer, or we can split them, and we can have both."

Taylor's mouth watered even as he picked up the pill. "Um, what is this?" he asked hesitantly. Still, he knew his mate wouldn't steer him wrong, so he popped it into his mouth and took a drink, swallowing it.

After Taylor had swallowed, Ulrick answered his question. "The alpha-mate of Jocomo's wolf pack, he's a doctor, worked with a scientist who's also part of the pack. They created that painkiller that works on shifters." Holding out a hand, Ulrick beckoned to him. "It should kick in pretty fast, judging by how it worked on Jocomo, so you'll be fairly comfortable while eating."

"Huh." Taylor slowly crossed to Ulrick and took his hand. "That's cool."

Taylor had always had to recover without the aid of medicine. To be able to get a little relief was a novel experience for him. Most human medicines just didn't work for a shifter because their metabolism burned through it too swiftly.

Threading their fingers together, Ulrick squeezed lightly. "Come on, Taylor. Jeremy only returned with the food fifteen minutes ago," he explained to him. "So everything's still hot."

Humming appreciatively, Taylor headed into the main room. He spotted Jeremy and Jocomo already seated at the table. They both had open cartons in front of them, and there were many more unopened ones.

"Hey, Jocomo," Taylor greeted, joining them at the table. "How are you feeling?"

The shifter was only wearing a pair of jogging shorts, leaving the extent of his injuries on display.

"Better now," Jocomo told him, even smiling at him before returning his attention to a large, rare steak that smelled absolutely amazing. "I hear you showed Ulrick where I was hidden, even after you were beaten damn near unconscious." Pausing with his fork close to his mouth, Jocomo added, "Thank you."

Gingerly taking his seat, Taylor felt a blush heat his cheeks. He didn't know what to say to that kind of praise. After clearing his throat, he flashed a smile the wolf shifter's way and told him, "Well, Ulrick was there to find you. I just got lucky to be his mate, so of course, I'd want to help him."

Jocomo swallowed his bite of food, still holding his gaze. "I think you would have helped him even if you weren't mates."

Taylor lost the fight against his blush, feeling the heat creep up his neck and through his cheeks.

"Thanks, babe," Ulrick stated, placing a container in front of him. "You did save me a hell of a lot of time." Then he opened it, revealing a huge burger. "Here's the onion rings and fries, too." Ulrick settled two containers in between them as he took his own seat before a partially eaten burger. "Enjoy."

"Thanks," Taylor responded, happy to have something else to focus on. Glancing over the table, he asked, "Is there a knife I could borrow? I'd like to cut my burger in half."

Taylor's mouth watered as anticipation filled him.

"Here." Jocomo pushed his knife toward Taylor.

Ulrick quickly grabbed it before sliding Taylor's carton toward him a little.

As Taylor watched Ulrick carefully cut his large bacon cheeseburger in half, he grabbed an onion ring. To his pleasure, he spotted a small tub of pinkish liquid in the container, too. Taylor squished the onion ring in half, making it thinner, then he dunked it in the fry sauce.

Biting off half the fry sauce-covered onion ring, Taylor closed his eyes in appreciation. He moaned softly with pleasure as he chewed the fried, fatty treat. Taylor was certain it had been years since he'd enjoyed them.

The mother-daughter couple who cooked for the alpha and his friends certainly never made onion rings. On occasion, they would bake French fries, but the inner circle always ate them all. Taylor had been forced to eat whatever was left behind by them, and that certainly didn't include what would be considered treats.

"I've heard you make those noises before, Taylor," Ulrick rumbled, his voice deep and husky. "But it wasn't while eating food."

Snapping his attention to his jaguar lover, Taylor gaped at Ulrick. He saw the hungry gleam in the bigger man's eyes, and his body flashed hot with answering desire. Then his stomach rumbled again.

Ulrick chuckled as he pushed Taylor's burger carton back

in front of him. "Eat, my mate," he encouraged. "We're expecting a call from Alpha Declan in an hour."

"Really?" Taylor grabbed a French fry and dunked an end in fry sauce. Unease slithered down his spine, squelching his earlier arousal. "Will he, um, will he be okay with me being your mate?" Before popping the tasty food into his mouth, Taylor couldn't help but admit his fears. "I'm not a wolf, and neither are you. Why would he help us? What will we do?"

"Alpha Declan'll help us," Ulrick assured, picking up his own burger. "I've been living with his pack for over a year now. They're the ones that taught me how to accept the animal I ended up with . . . helped me learn to communicate with him and coexist." With a shrug, Ulrick added, "And shift super-fast."

"You do shift really fast." Taylor carefully picked up half his burger. "Um, can you explain what you meant when you told me you weren't born a shifter, but made one?"

"What?" Jeremy snapped his attention away from his massive Cobb salad. He glanced between them, lettuce dropping from his fork as he froze. "How's that possible?"

As they ate, Ulrick explained what had happened. He told how he was originally a human special forces soldier. He'd been injured on his last mission, and when he'd been shipped home, the general he'd been reporting to had entered him into an illegal experimentation program. Somehow, those scientists had managed to figure out how to splice shifter genes into a human. While they'd kept him on drugs to keep the cat in check so he didn't shift, they'd also done some kind of chemical mind-wipe. Ulrick hadn't been able to start thinking for himself until his handler disappeared.

"What happened to him?" Taylor asked softly. "What if he shows up again?" He paused with an onion ring hovering over his carton. "Could he hit you with those drugs again and take you away from me?"

Ulrick narrowed his eyes as he peered intently at Taylor. "That will *never* happen," he stated firmly. "The doctors and vampires in Stone Ridge have worked hard to fix my brain." Barking a laugh, Ulrick added, "And now that I'm actually one with my jaguar, we would both fight tooth and nail to always be by your side."

Taylor nodded slowly as he smiled back at Ulrick. "I'll fight to stay by your side, too." With a growl filling his voice, he declared, "I may not be a big coyote, but if your asshole handler ever showed up again, I'd find a way to rip out his throat."

"You wouldn't be alone in that," Jocomo claimed, scooping up a forkful of mac and cheese. Before popping it into his mouth, he told him, "You're part of the pack, Ulrick, even if you don't believe us." Jocomo shrugged and muttered around his mouthful, "You got plenty a friends who'll fight for ya, too."

Ulrick chuckled, looking as if he hadn't considered that. "Thanks, man."

Once the meals were polished off, they moved to the living area. While Taylor and Jocomo couldn't really relax in the cushy chairs, the pain meds made it so they were at least comfortable. Taylor sat perched on a soft sofa cushion next to Ulrick as they tried to find something to watch on TV. They'd just decided on an adventure movie when Ulrick's phone rang. His mate muted the TV and answered it.

"Hello, Alpha Declan," Ulrick greeted. "Is it okay to put you on speaker?"

"Certainly." The deep voice had a hint of an Irish accent. "Ye're with shifters, so they'll be able to hear anyway if ye're in the same room."

"We are," Ulrick confirmed before pushing a button on the phone. "After the pain meds, Jocomo and Taylor were well enough to join us at the table for a big meal."

"I'm glad to hear it," Alpha Declan claimed. "I received the pictures ye sent, Ulrick." A growl entered the alpha's voice as he continued, "There'll be heavy restitution from them for their treatment of you, Jocomo."

"But they won't pay it," Taylor whispered, meeting Jeremy's gaze. "They'll make the pack pay, instead."

"Is that Taylor?" the alpha asked.

Taylor flinched, ducking his head. "Um, yes, Alpha." He really should have known better than to open his mouth.

"Try to relax, Taylor," Alpha Declan encouraged, his voice filling with unexpected warmth. "I can practically hear yer tension in just those few words."

Ulrick reached over and settled his hand on Taylor's thigh, rubbing lightly. "Declan won't censure you for expressing your opinion, babe," he assured. Leaning over, Ulrick pecked a kiss to his temple. "Why do you say that they won't pay the restitution themselves? If they don't, it'll bring the shifter council down on their heads."

Taylor exchanged another look with Jeremy, who grimaced while rubbing the back of his neck.

He's probably thinking the same thing.

"Well, as the alpha, beta, and head enforcer, they think everyone else in the pack is there to serve them." Taylor tried to explain the men's behavior, even if he didn't agree with it. "That means, if they have to pay a fine or whatever, then they'll make sure that the money comes from the pack." Meeting Ulrick's gaze, Taylor added, "And because it was Jocomo that brought attention to them, they'll make his parents come up with most of it."

Alpha Declan hummed, obviously pondering what Taylor had said. "Then we'll have to make certain the restitution we ask for isn't something they can fob on their people," he commented gravely. "Jocomo, can ye walk me through who chained ye up, as well as who tortured ye?"

Blowing out a breath, Jocomo nodded even though he

probably knew that Alpha Declan couldn't see it. "I was having dinner with Jeremy and my mother when my father arrived with Enforcer Kris," he began slowly. "They escorted me to the pack house, where Alpha Stewart ordered me to be chained up for spreading radical ideology."

"Radical ideology?" Alpha Declan repeated, cutting in. "If ye don't mind me asking, what were ye saying?"

Scoffing, Jocomo shared, "Just that there was nothing wrong with Jeremy's desire to explore possible alternatives to the standard male-female pairings. That Fate has given plenty of shifters a fated mate of the same sex." Rolling his eyes, Jocomo grumbled, "I guess I shouldn't have made that comment to a guy named Laurence."

Jeremy groaned. "Laurence is an ass-kisser," he explained, and Taylor found himself nodding in agreement. "He'll look for any way to get in better with the inner circle. He must have told them."

"I overheard Alpha Stewart talking with Kris about rewarding Laurence for his loyalty by training him in enforcer duties." Taylor shuddered just at the idea of Laurence in a position of power. "He's a bully, though. He'd totally take advantage of his position."

"Well, like gravitates to like," Alpha Declan grumbled. "Alpha Stewart and his friends are obviously doing the same thing." The alpha's sigh came through the line before he asked, "And the beatings, Jocomo. Who issued them?"

"Mostly, it was Beta Friar," Jocomo shared, looking at the healing bruises on his thighs. "But the alpha did issue the first one. Said I was being punished for spreading lies. Enforcer Kris liked to stand around, watch and laugh, but he never actually struck me with anything but his words and indifference."

"Hmmm," Alpha Declan mused. "I'll pass that information on to the shifter council enforcer that's going to show up at yer door in two days."

Taylor gaped.

Who's coming here?

"When and who should we expect, Alpha?" Ulrick asked, continuing to rub Taylor's thigh soothingly. "Anyone you've met before?"

"Actually, yes," Alpha Declan revealed. "Ye'll be visited by Head Enforcer Mycroft Portent. He was escorting Councilman Regales to Louisiana." The alpha let out a chuckle. "Guess Alpha Kontra's currently staying there, and he and his were helping the CIA nail down a mole in their organization. The councilman wanted first-hand knowledge of the incident."

Gaping, Taylor glanced at the men around the room. He saw Jeremy appeared just as surprised. The other pair didn't even bat an eyelash as Alpha Declan name-dropped head enforcers and councilmen.

Just damn. These guys are connected.

"I believe Eli's going to be joinin' Mycroft, so he can check ye both out," Declan continued as if he hadn't just shocked Taylor—not that the alpha would know. "Eli's a shifter doctor. His mate, Sam, is a nurse, and they'll make certain neither of ye end up with any lasting effects." Before anyone could say anything, Declan continued, "Oh, and one more thing. Ulrick, ye should really complete yer bond with Taylor. That way his ex-alpha will have no possible claim to him."

Claim to me? What's that mean?

Taylor snapped his attention to Ulrick, wondering how his shifter would take essentially being ordered to claim him.

Ulrick's grin appeared feral, hungry. "Alpha, it would be my genuine pleasure."

Heat of a different nature rushed through Taylor, and his dick went ramrod straight in his shorts.

Chapter Nine

As Ulrick finished up the call with Declan, he struggled with keeping his mind on the alpha and his words. From Taylor's shocked scent, he figured it was a big deal that the wolf shifter knew not only the head enforcer for the shifter council, but a councilman, as well. Ulrick figured he would keep his mouth shut—at least for a little while—that the alpha had actually stood before the council and helped overthrow the wolf shifter representative.

Ulrick had heard the story secondhand, since it had happened a few years before.

When Ulrick had decided to drive east, he hadn't given any thought to the possibility of driving through or near the territories of other shifters . . . or even vampires. From what he'd learned through the Stone Ridge grapevine, gargoyles were just as reclusive as shifters, living deep in obscurity. Like shifter packs, they didn't mind using the guise of a religious commune or even a nudist colony to keep most folks away.

As soon as Ulrick said their goodbyes to the alpha wolf shifter, he pushed any thought of him and those that were coming to visit to the back of his mind. He found his attention riveted on Taylor. While Ulrick desperately wanted to do exactly as the alpha wolf had suggested, he was coming up blank on how to get it done.

Well, of course Ulrick knew how to do it. He'd been having sex with both women and men since he'd figured out how to sweet talk a lady out of her panties at the age of fourteen. What Ulrick wasn't certain about was the best way to go about it when Taylor's back and thighs were covered in painful welts.

After all, painkillers could only overcome so much.

"Well, you guys have a great evening," Jocomo teased with a smirk. Lifting his hand, he wiggled his fingers as he focused on Jeremy. "Give me the remote, bro. I'm ready for a little mindless television."

Jeremy scoffed as he handed over said remote. "Sure, but only if you pick something that we can turn up really loud." Smirking, he winked at Taylor. "With plenty of explosions."

Grinning broadly, Jocomo quipped, "Is there any other kind?" Then he sobered and peered at Ulrick. "Uh, I forgot to ask earlier. Will I be okay to take another painkiller before bed in an hour or two?"

Ulrick hesitated, racking his brain for any information Lark had given him on the pills. He really couldn't remember any warnings. Focusing on Jocomo, he shrugged.

"To be honest, I can't recall anything," Ulrick admitted. "Do you want my phone so you can text Lark?"

Shaking his head, Jocomo smiled at him. "Naw. If the alpha-mate wasn't too worried about telling you, I'm sure it'll be fine."

Ulrick nodded before helping Taylor to his feet. "Want anything before we head to the bedroom?" he asked, even though his dick was hard as nails, making it tough to think.

"Another bottle of water." Then he gaped. "Oh. We totally forgot to cut the blueberry pie."

Watching Taylor hesitate, his gaze straying to the counter, Ulrick almost thought the coyote shifter would ask for some. Then he shook his head and gave him a shy smile. "Maybe later." His eyelids slipped to half-mast as he whispered, "After we work up an appetite."

With a growl, Ulrick jerked a nod. He slid his arm around Taylor's shoulders and began guiding him to their bedroom.

As he ushered his cute coyote inside and closed the door behind him, Ulrick still hadn't figured out how he was going to make claiming Taylor as pain-free as possible.

As Ulrick headed toward the bed, he froze. An unexpected thought pushed into his brain. It wasn't something he'd ever considered before, but the idea could work.

"Is everything okay?" Taylor had turned and was peering at him with his arms crossed over his chest, gripping the opposite elbows with his hands. "We don't have to do this right away, if you don't want to."

Growling under his breath, Ulrick closed the several steps between them, uncertain when Taylor had managed to get so far away. He'd obviously been way too stuck in his head. Holding his coyote's gaze, Ulrick rested his hands on the smaller man's shoulders.

"My dick is threatening to break off, it's so hard," Ulrick declared, staring into Taylor's gorgeous hazel eyes. "The only reason I didn't take you in the shower was because you were injured. I would have sunk my teeth into your neck at the waterfall, but you stopped me." That reminder gave Ulrick pause. "Perhaps it's you who doesn't want me." The thought caused an uneasy twist in his gut, and his jaguar growled in his mind. Still, Ulrick had to get to the bottom of whatever was going on in Taylor's brain. "Is that it? Are you not ready for me to claim you?"

"No!" Taylor shook his head rapidly as he gripped Ulrick's upper arms. "That's not it at all." Staring beseechingly at him, he told him, "My reason at the waterfall made sense, just like yours did in the shower." After a second of nibbling his bottom lip, Taylor continued, "But like you, I'm really not sure what the best position would be for you to take me. I mean, my back and thighs can't handle lying on my back, or being on my hands and knees so you can fuck me, or me riding you." Taylor released him in favor of wringing his hands. "I just . . . the painkillers help, but I don't think—" He stopped and shook his head.

Ulrick nodded slowly, having had all those thoughts himself. Seeing the way Taylor's shoulders slumped, coupled with his disappointed sigh, told Ulrick that his mate had misunderstood. Lowering his hands to his waist and popping the button on his fly, Ulrick was only too happy to rectify that assumption.

"Get undressed, Taylor," Ulrick ordered gently. Seeing Taylor's confused expression, he told him, "Just because I can't fuck you doesn't mean that *you* can't fuck *me*."

As Ulrick had expected, Taylor gaped at him.

Smirking, Ulrick eased down his zipper, allowing his hard rod free of the confining fabric. "Come on," he teased, beginning to push the fabric down his legs. "Surly you must have thought about it."

Taylor quickly shook his head. "Not once," he admitted, even as his gaze riveted on Ulrick's hard flesh. "A-Always thought you would top me."

"Oh, I still will, my coyote shifter," Ulrick assured, offering Taylor a lazy grin. "Probably daily . . . or even several times a day." With a husky chuckle just thinking about it, Ulrick rumbled, "But, like I told you in the shower, I won't claim you until I'm certain I won't tear open your wounds." After shucking his jeans, he stood before Taylor in the buff. "That means, you need to claim me."

Ulrick watched Taylor's chest rise and fall quickly for several heartbeats. His cute coyote's gaze roved over his body, as if he couldn't decide what to settle on. In truth, Ulrick loved that response, and he flexed and relaxed certain muscles for his lover's pleasure—from his pectorals, biceps, abdominals, and even his thighs.

When Taylor whimpered, the smell of his need flooding the room with its heady pleasantness, Ulrick decided it was time to get the party started.

Stepping forward, Ulrick gently gripped the waistband of Taylor's sweatpants. He made a mental note to take his lover shopping for some new threads once they ended up settled. Ulrick had the insane urge to lavish his mate with comfort, as well as nice things.

"Is that something you'd be interested in doing?" Ulrick asked softly as he eased to one knee. Peering up at his coyote, he tugged the front of the shorts forward and down to reveal Taylor's slender prick. The lovely piece of meat was damn near perfectly proportioned to his shifter's body, leaning just a smidge on the long side. "Would you like to fuck and claim me, Taylor?"

As Ulrick asked the all-important question, he wrapped his hands around to the back of his waistband. He tucked his thumbs into the band and pulled it several inches away from his flesh. Ulrick began using his hold to lower the shorts, first past the glorious mounds he had every intention of sampling—it would just be a couple more days—and down the man's legs, being certain not to touch his thighs in the process.

"Y-Yes," Taylor finally answered him, stepping out of the shorts. "Oh, gods. Yes. I want us bonded so badly."

Even as he answered in the affirmative, he still sounded uncertain.

"What is it, my mate?" Ulrick asked as he returned to his feet. Resting his hands on Taylor's shoulders, he massaged them lightly, just as he'd noticed his mate enjoyed. "Talk to me, babe. Please."

Ulrick had never begged a day in his life, but for his mate, he would do it . . . sort of. He didn't really consider that begging so much as being polite. There was maybe some prodding in there, too.

"I-I've never topped before," Taylor finally admitted to him after a moment of nibbling on his bottom lip. Peering at him through his lashes, he quietly asked, "What if I'm not any good?"

While it was a close thing, Ulrick managed to bite back his bark of laughter. He didn't want to belittle his lover, after all. Instead, he lifted a hand to Taylor's jaw and skimmed his thumb along the smooth, hard line there.

Considering Ulrick hadn't seen Taylor shave, he figured his sweet coyote was just naturally mostly hairless.

Ulrick really liked that.

"Oh, my sweet, beautiful coyote." Ulrick wasn't usually one for compliments, platitudes, and honorifics, but with Taylor, he just couldn't stop himself. After all, he loved the sweet smile or gorgeous blush his compliments caused. Holding Taylor's gaze, Ulrick told him, "You are my mate. Anything that we do together will be one-hundred-percent *perfect*."

"You think so?" Taylor looked so damn hopeful as he met his gaze.

Nodding confidently, Ulrick claimed, "I've seen plenty of Stone Ridge wolves find their fated mate, and while they'd all had bumps, just like us, it's worked out for them." He smirked and rolled his eyes, unable to help himself. "Plus, they're always all over each other every chance they can get. I know anything we do together will be damn perfect, baby."

Taylor nodded once. "Okay." His smile once again turned shy. "I trust you."

"Thank you," Ulrick replied, suddenly feeling as if he stood ten feet tall. After all, his sweet mate had been beaten, battered, and taken advantage of for years. Having Taylor's trust made Ulrick's heart beat just a little bit faster. Unable to help himself, he admitted, "You truly honor me."

"You saved me," Taylor murmured with a sweet smile. Then his expression grew hungry. "And there's no way I'll ever deny the amazing gift the Fates have given me in a sexy, amazing, perfect mate like you."

A low growl of pleasure and need escaped Ulrick, and his jaguar mentally urged him to get his ass in gear. He was in complete agreement with his animal.

Dipping his head, Ulrick pecked a kiss to Taylor's lips. He knew he would be happy to spend hours exploring his mate's mouth, but he had other things on his mind first. Ulrick eased away and crossed to the nightstand. When Ulrick had placed the lube in there, he'd never thought he'd be using it on himself . . . well, except for lubing up his dick.

Ulrick settled on the bed on his back before popping the cap on the lube. As he poured a good dollop onto his fingers, he watched Taylor climb onto the bed beside him. His lover settled on his side as Ulrick handed him the lube.

"Grease up, my coyote shifter," Ulrick encouraged, flicking his attention to his lover's pole. "You're gonna go deep." Scoffing, he murmured, "I'm sure I'll like how it feels."

From rumors, Ulrick knew that on very rare occasions, even Alpha Declan switched things up with his mate.

"O-Okay."

Taylor did as he'd been bidden, even as Ulrick spread his legs and reached between them. Without preamble, he pushed his middle finger deep into his channel. Before being changed, every once in a while, Ulrick had fingered himself, but it had been a long damn time, and he immediately felt the sting.

Still, Ulrick managed to bite back his grimace. Instead, he focused on Taylor, admiring the way his lover—soon-to-be partner and mate—was slicking up his erection. For the first time in his life, as Ulrick finger-fucked himself, he felt his mouth water.

Damn. I actually want to taste my coyote's erection.

Ulrick had never sucked a cock in his life, and he'd never been tempted to.

Something else new to try with him.

Smiling at Taylor, Ulrick gave him a sultry smile, doing his best to ignore the nerves that were threatening to cause his erection to flag. He teased over his prostate as he eased a second finger in beside the first. Ulrick had zero desire for his vulnerable coyote to know just how nervous he was.

"You're so fucking sexy, lying there touching yourself," Ulrick declared, earning a blush from his lover. As soon as he'd managed to grow accustomed to three fingers inside him—mostly anyway—Ulrick pulled them out and beckoned. "Come here, Taylor."

Even as Taylor began to ease closer to him, he murmured, "It's easier on your stomach if it's been a while."

Ulrick grinned, showing plenty of teeth. "But I can't claim you that way, my coyote." He wasn't about to tell Taylor that this was his first time receiving. Instead, Ulrick demanded, "Get over here and fuck me, my mate."

To Ulrick's pleasure—and relief—Taylor obeyed, slipping between his spread thighs. He knew he couldn't grip his back, so he settled his palms on his lover's ass instead. The firm mounds felt perfect cradled in his palms.

I'll enjoy holding them while pounding into him, too.

Then Taylor guided his greased cock head to Ulrick's prepared hole, and he just remembered to breathe while pushing out.

As Ulrick felt Taylor slide not just his cock deep inside him, but his teeth into his neck, he knew it was the best decision he'd ever made.

CHAPTER TEN

Taylor watched with a mixture of awe and trepidation as his coyote's pack lands appeared up ahead. Gripping the sides of Ulrick's leather jacket, he did his best to remember that he was not alone. Fortunately, it was easy considering the number of motorcycles that surrounded them.

A day prior, Taylor had been shocked when Head Enforcer Mycroft Portent had arrived with his vampire mate, Boyd Johnson. They'd only been mated a short while, but the love between them had been amazing to see. Plus, Boyd was the first vampire Taylor had ever met.

They'd been accompanied by Doctor Eli Raetz, a python shifter. The man's small wolf shifter mate had accompanied him and acted as his nurse. The pair had assessed them both with kind professionalism.

Four others had been part of the group. There was a white tiger shifter named Adam, who'd spent most of his time crooning at Jeremy's truck while fixing all her mechanical problems. Adam's mate was a moose shifter named Noah, who seemed inordinately great at anticipating what tools Adam would need.

The last two were also a mated pair. Ronald was Noah's younger brother—Ronnie, he'd asked to be called—but he was a damn dominant and huge male who looked far older than his twenty-three years, making him a great escort for a shifter council enforcer. The last man was Hector, an armadillo shifter. The Mexican male was older than Ronnie, helping to soothe the aggressive shifter, and also knew how to shoot, keeping a revolver hidden in an ankle holster.

Taylor hoped that, someday, he would have at least a fraction of the self-confidence they exuded.

As the group roared down the road, Taylor noticed the ruined grass and gravel, telling him where Ulrick had shot out a tire on Alpha Stewart's SUV, sending him off the road. Passing that an instant later, he spotted a red blotch on the ground. Taylor figured that was Beta Friar's spilled blood, but he couldn't dredge up even a drop of sympathy.

The shifter's an asshole.

Even partially healed, Taylor still felt the occasional twinge in his back and legs. Only the group's assurance that he would be completely safe the entire time had convinced him to return to pack lands. Taylor could have spent the next several hundred years never seeing those leaders again.

Unfortunately, as the speaker of the accused, Ulrick had to attend the meeting. Jocomo also accompanied them, but he sat in the passenger seat of the pick-up truck. Jeremy drove, as they intended to return the vehicle so it didn't end up as a theft on their record—should their father decide to report it as stolen.

So far, according to Alpha Declan's sources, he hadn't, but they didn't know if that would change unless it was returned. If all went well, Jeremy and Jocomo would be leaving on the motorcycle that Hector was riding. Evidently, the armadillo shifter usually rode behind Ronnie, but they'd picked up the large *Harley* so they'd have an extra ride for them.

"Try to relax," Ulrick urged, reaching back and patting Taylor's leg. "Gods willing, we'll be in and out within an hour."

Taylor nodded, doing his best to calm down. He sure hoped things went smoothly.

"Well, it looks like someone gave us away." Adam's deep voice came through the microphone of the helmet Taylor wore. He hadn't even known that was a thing as he heard the tiger shifter continue, "It seems these guys are waiting for us."

"Even if the entire pack attacked, there's no way they could take us," Ronnie muttered dismissively. "No offense, coyotes."

"None taken," Taylor replied, since he knew that Jeremy probably hadn't heard the comment due to driving the truck. "Um, d-does this change, uh, anything?"

"Not by much," Mycroft replied with warmth in his tone. "It may even speed things up because we don't have to wait for the inner circle to be gathered for us."

As Mycroft parked his leopard-painted bullet bike—Taylor had heard the markings were damn similar to the print of his cat's fur—Alpha Stewart moved to the middle of the pack house's main steps. He crossed his arms over his chest imposingly and glared at the group. As he swept his attention over the assembled men, his lips twitched, but the alpha somehow managed to keep from sneering.

Instead of flanking him as was usual, Beta Friar stood off to the right. On his left thigh, a bandage could just be seen at the hem of the cargo shorts he wore. Friar leaned against the railing, his damaged leg cocked up. His thick arms were crossed over his chest, and he glared at the assembling group.

It was Head Enforcer Kris who flanked the alpha's right shoulder. His dark eyes were narrowed, and his expression remained bland. Only the slight pinching around his lips told Taylor that he was not at all pleased with having the group assembled there.

"I scent that you're shifters," Alpha Stewart declared, sweeping his gaze over them. He was probably trying to figure out who the leader was. "Declare yourselves before I take your arrival as a declaration of aggression."

Head Enforcer Mycroft removed his helmet and lifted his chin as he eyed the alpha coolly. "Hello. You're Alpha Steward, I take it?" He rested the helmet on a handlebar before swinging his leg over the front, dismounting the bike. "I'm Head Enforcer Mycroft Portent, and I work for the shifter council."

"Shifter Council," Beta Friar cut in with a sneer. "What the fuck would you be doing here?"

As the beta spoke, a number of the others dismounted as well. When Ulrick urged Taylor to do the same, he obeyed.

Just as Mycroft began, "Well," Ulrick dismounted while removing his helmet.

Friar cut in, roaring, "You!" He pointed at Ulrick. "That's him, Alpha. That's the bastard who kidnapped our people and shot me!"

Rolling his eyes, Ulrick smirked as he helped Taylor remove his helmet. "A little hard for me to kidnap your people when I wasn't the one doing the driving, don't you think, Beta Friar?" He set Taylor's helmet on the motorcycle's seat before wrapping his arm around Taylor's shoulders in a protective and possessive move that nobody missed. "I'm here representing the Stone Ridge wolf pack on Jocomo's behalf. He's here for restitution."

"Restitution," Beta Friar snarled. "We don't owe—"

"That's enough, Beta Friar," Alpha Stewart declared, cutting him off. His look was sharp, and his words curt.

Beta Friar didn't look pleased, but he shut up.

Wow, never seen dissension between them like that before.

In the past, the trio had always been a unit, supporting each other in all things.

Taylor wondered what trickery this was. Then he felt as if his skin began to crawl as he spotted the way Alpha Stewart eyed him. Instead of speaking to him, the alpha returned his focus to Mycroft.

"Thank you for returning our missing coyote shifters," Alpha Stewart stated, glancing toward Jeremy to include him. "And our truck." Indicating the front door, he stated, "Perhaps we should head into the office for some coffee. You can explain your comment about restitution."

"No, thank you, Alpha Stewart," Mycroft replied cooly. He glanced around at the pack members, who were blatantly lingering about and eavesdropping. "This is not something that should be kept behind closed doors."

Alpha Stewart's eyes narrowed. Beta Friar curled his lips into a deep sneer. Even Enforcer Kris frowned just a little as he glanced at the alpha as if seeking direction.

Tipping his chin up as if he were looking down on Mycroft, Stewart stated, "Very well, Enforcer Mycroft. Let's get this over with." He swept his gaze over the area, frowning at those loitering about. Raising his voice, Stewart declared, "As I'm certain we *all* have things we need to be doing."

Oddly enough, only a few people scurried away.

Huh. What's going on with that?

Taylor couldn't remember the last time one person, let alone several, hadn't jumped to obey even a veiled order from Alpha Stewart.

"In accordance with shifter law, Alpha Stewart," Mycroft began to drone coldly, redrawing everyone's attention. "You, your beta, and your head enforcer have been found guilty of crimes against a member of another pack, who was under the safety of the visiting family ruling and was untouchable to violence or holding." Crossing his arms over his chest, Mycroft arched one brow. "Acting under your orders, your beta administered nearly fatal damage to the wolf shifter, Jocomo. While you and your head enforcer will be sanctioned, restitution to be determined by Jocomo's alpha, your beta will be stripped of his position and taken into custody. You will—"

"Wait just a damn minute," Beta Friar roared, limping forward. "You can't do that. You have no authorization over our pack's inner workings. You—"

"Shifter law is clear," Mycroft cut in, scowling at Friar. "Had there been a problem, the worst you should have done was banish him from your territory." Holding up an envelope, which Taylor knew held physical pictures of how Ulrick had found Jocomo, Mycroft continued, "No behavior would ever justify a shifter being found in this condition on your lands."

"How we deal with our criminals is no concern of—" Beta Friar tried again.

"Enough," Alpha Stewart snapped, glaring at Friar. "Sorry, Friar. You *will* go with these men." Upon seeing Friar's shocked look, Stewart stated coldly, "Your usefulness has come to an end." Dismissing a clearly uncomprehending Friar, the alpha turned his glare on Taylor. "Head into the house, Taylor. We'll discuss your actions later."

"Not a fucking chance," Ulrick declared, tucking Taylor tighter against him. "Taylor is *my* fated mate. We've claimed each other. He's coming with me."

Scoffing, Alpha Stewart took on a look of disgust. "Fate doesn't pair those of the same sex. They couldn't propagate, leaving a pack weak and—"

"Oh, good grief," Adam cut in, sounding bored. Using his thumb, he pointed at the alpha. "This attitude again?"

Ronnie rolled his eyes as he snorted. "Really, dude?" The huge moose shifter shook his head. "What? Are you stuck in the dark ages?"

With a snicker, while cuddled close to Eli's side, Sam commented, "Yeah. Ever hear of artificial insemination?"

While Alpha Stewart's face had become darker and darker with obvious rage, he didn't get a chance to comment.

Beside him, Friar roared, "You'd dare betray me?"

Before the alpha could respond, Friar lunged for him while shifting. The beta might have only been half-coyote when he landed on Stewart, but he'd managed to form his claws. As Friar continued to transition to his coyote, he scratched and clawed at Stewart's throat.

Friar had just managed to gain his canine mouth and had wrapped his jaws around Stewart's throat when Kris finally responded. In human form, he wrapped his arms around Friar's torso. Kris heaved and yanked, tearing Friar away from Stewart.

Blood sprayed across the porch planking, and Stewart gurgled as he weakly slapped a hand over his torn-out throat. A few seconds later, while Kris was still grappling with Friar, Stewart's hand flopped to the decking, and his eyes glazed in death.

"Separate them," Mycroft grumbled, shaking his head with disgust.

Adam snickered before charging forward. Eli was right next to him. Without bothering to undress, the big blond jumped and shifted in mid-air. A massive white tiger landed on the struggling pair.

Even as Adam's tiger batted Friar's coyote out of Kris's arms, a massive python slithered onto the porch. The long slender beast twisted around the porch ceiling's latices before swooping Kris up in his coils. Eli easily incapacitated the coyote shifter, who continued to stare angrily at Friar—while the now-ex-beta had been pinned by Adam's tiger with one huge paw. The tiger even had his tongue hanging out as if he was having the most fun in ages.

"Damn," Ulrick grumbled, glaring and shaking his head. "I really wanted to help take those fuckers out."

"Don't feel bad, man," Noah stated, patting Ulrick on the back. "Adam thinks this is playtime. I wouldn't have thought of trying to stop him."

"I get it." Ulrick still shook his head. "Doesn't make me happier about it."

"Well, this creates a problem." Mycroft strode up the porch steps, stepping over Stewart's body with nary a glance. Scowling between the other two, he crossed his arms over his chest. "Now I gotta stick around and figure out who the fuck should take over the pack."

Taylor couldn't help but think that the leopard shifter did not look pleased.

"Um, Enforcer Mycroft?" Jeremy called, even going so far as to raise his hand hesitantly. "M-Maybe I could stick around and help?" The big coyote shifter actually blushed as he muttered, "I mean, I do know everyone here."

Mycroft grinned broadly at Jeremy. "Perfect." He clapped his hands together as he peered around the group. "Have Ronnie and Hector help you gather your things from your parents' home. You'll stay with me in the pack house for the duration."

Jeremy looked relieved as he nodded. "Thank you, sir."

"I'll stay, too," Jocomo declared, his eyes narrowed. "I don't know them as much anymore," he admitted as he gripped Jeremy's neck and squeezed in a brotherly way. "But I ain't lettin' you outta my sight for a bit, bro."

In Taylor's opinion, Jeremy looked relieved.

"What about you, babe?" Ulrick asked, touching his chin with his fingertips. "Is there anything here you need before we go?" Then he cocked his head and asked, "Or did you want to stick around? Is there someone you want to, uh, say goodbye to?"

Peering up at Ulrick from beneath his lashes, Taylor smiled at his mate's thoughtfulness. "No, I'm good," he told him. Tucking himself against his lover's chest, he rested his hands on Ulrick's impressive pectorals. "I'm happy to head out whenever you want and go wherever you'd like."

Ulrick growled softly, his eyes narrowing. "I recall you saying that you hadn't traveled much."

Taylor shook his head while nibbling his bottom lip.

"Well, I think a few weeks on the road with nothing but you and my bike are in order." Ulrick's tone turned husky.

"What do you say?"

With his breath catching in his chest, Taylor nodded quickly. "Yes, please?" He felt a bit of heat rise in his cheeks as he asked, "C-Can we go to Yellowstone? I've always wanted to see Old Faithful." After a second, Taylor added, "And buffalo."

"That sounds damn perfect," Ulrick replied before pecking a kiss to Taylor's lips. A second later, he swung back aboard the motorcycle and handed Taylor his helmet. "Let's get the hell out of dodge, baby."

Excitement coursing through Taylor for the first time in . . . more years than he wanted to admit, he grabbed his helmet, slipped it onto his head, and swung up behind Ulrick. As his mate turned the motorcycle around and started them away from the pack that hadn't really been Taylor's home in nearly a decade, he waved to the friendly guys who'd helped him as anticipation thrummed through him.

Finally, I get to start my life.

About the Author

Charlie started writing fantasy when she was eight, and after stumbling onto her first erotic romance at age nineteen, she realized her true calling. She now focuses on writing gay erotic romance, normally of the paranormal variety, with heroes of all kinds. With the help and support of her husband, Charlie finally fulfilled one of her life-long goals . . . move to acreage with her horses. You can often find her curled up with her laptop and a cup of tea or glass of wine, creating her next adventure. Charlie enjoys exploring the mountains of her new Oregon home on horseback, 4-wheeler, or motorcycle.

She can be reached at ch.richards2010@yahoo.com

Or visit her at www.charlie-richards.com.

www.ingramcontent.com/pod-product-compliance
Lightning Source LLC
LaVergne TN
LVHW020654100826
845148LV00012B/2483

9781487439354